PRAISE F
THE DOT MEYERHO

"Riveting, compelling, and authentic! Ellen Kirschman's been-there, done-that experience makes this a real standout."

—Hank Phillippi Ryan,
Agatha, Anthony, and Mary Higgins Clark Awards winner

"Psychological thriller writing at its finest."

—DP Lyle, award-winning author
of the Jake Longly, Dub Walker, and Samantha Cody thriller series

"A deftly crafted novel of compelling complexity . . . *Burying Ben* is an inherently absorbing read from beginning to end and marks author Ellen Kirschman as a novelist of exceptional storytelling talent."

—*Midwest Book Review*

"Kirschman . . . perceptively treats complex racial, feminist, personal, and political issues while providing intimate knowledge of cops' shop procedure."

—*Publishers Weekly*

THE ANSWER TO HIS PRAYERS

The Answer to His Prayers

A Dot Meyerhoff Mystery

Ellen Kirschman

ISBN: 978-1-5040-9420-7

This edition published in 2024 by Open Road Integrated Media, Inc.
180 Maiden Lane
New York, NY 10038
www.openroadmedia.com

Emergency dispatchers are unsung heroes rarely receiving the acknowledgment or support they deserve. This book is dedicated to them.

THE ANSWER TO HIS PRAYERS

1

Nothing good happens at two in the morning. Which is why I am driving through Kenilworth's deserted streets—my face still creased with sleep, my body still warm from Frank's and my bed—to meet a 911 dispatcher who has just taken the worst call of her professional life.

I turn into the nearly empty parking lot behind police headquarters and find a space next to the back steps. Three rookies, still young, still eager, burst out the door and race past me to their patrol cars. The midnight shift is their playground. All crooks and no brass.

Raylene Sibley, the communications manager, is waiting for me at the door. It's the middle of the night for her too, only she looks like she just stepped off the cover of *Vogue* in a black pantsuit with a huge scarlet collar. Her hair and make-up perfect. "This way," she says and starts down the hall. She's a big woman who moves with a ballerina's grace. I have to push to keep up.

"Wendy's in the break room. She wants to go home, but I was afraid to let her leave until you checked her out. She's a sweet kid, only twenty-three. And pretty. Oh, Lord. The minute she started working here there was a slew of officers wandering in and out of the comm center just to look." She takes a deep breath.

"I pulled the dispatch tape as soon as I got in. I could barely stand to listen to it. The caller was a disabled man in a wheelchair living in a mobile home. Debris in the road slowed the fire engines. By the time they got there, the trailer was engulfed in flames and they couldn't open the door. Wendy, bless her heart, stayed on the phone, talking to the victim as he burned to death."

I've never met Wendy. I have no way of predicting how she might react to this trauma. My job is to conduct pre-employment psychological screening for the cops and provide counseling after critical incidents. I have repeatedly asked Chief Pence to let me screen dispatchers too. He nixes the idea every time Raylene or I bring it up. Dispatchers don't carry guns, so he thinks it's sufficient to hire them on the basis of background checks alone. We stop in front of the break room. Raylene lowers her voice to a whisper.

"Wendy works hard. Takes every overtime shift she can. Never a discipline problem. Shows up for work on time. Doesn't ask for special treatment. Always cheerful."

"Personal life?"

"I'm her supervisor. If she's got one, she wouldn't talk to me about it."

Wendy is sitting upright on the edge of a hard leather cot. She looks younger than twenty-three, dressed in a boxy white sweater and skinny jeans. Her long streaky blonde hair falls in springy coils in front of her face until she pushes it back behind her tiny ears, revealing cornflower blue eyes. She is, as Raylene said, very pretty. Delicate and pale as though she'd stepped out of a medieval tapestry, one hand on a harp, the other on a unicorn. She stands, pulls her sweater down past her hips. She's slim. Gaining weight is an occupational hazard for dispatchers. High stress, low activity, rotten hours, and a banquet of fatty foods at the ready. Extra helpings of anything in a police station —cookies, cake, pizza—all wind up in the dispatch center and eventually around the dispatchers' waists.

"Hello Wendy. I'm Dr. Dot Meyerhoff, the department psychologist. I understand that you've just been through an extraordinarily challenging incident." I extend my hand. She shakes it. Her palm is warm and sweaty.

"Am I in trouble?"

Raylene places her hand on Wendy's shoulder. "Any time there's a critical incident, we call Dr. Meyerhoff to debrief whoever was involved. Strictly protocol. You're not in trouble. I just want to make sure you're okay. Dr. Meyerhoff will talk to you about the call and how it might affect you over the next few days. She knows a great deal about trauma and critical incident stress. Feel free to say whatever you want; it will just be between the two of you." She closes the door behind her.

Wendy gives me a nervous smile, her tiny white teeth brilliant in the dim light. I pull up a chair next to the cot leaving just enough space to give us both some room. I know from experience that counseling someone who has just gone through a terrible trauma is the equivalent of being exposed to secondhand smoke: their pain seeps into my pores and sticks to my clothes.

"I already told Raylene what happened."

"I'm not so much wanting to know what happened, Wendy, but how it's affecting you personally."

She pulls a hank of hair over her shoulder, examining each whorling strand for split ends.

"I'm fine. Just tired. I'd like to go home, please."

I'm not surprised. Humans are meant to work during the day, sleep at night, keep regular routines, and get adequate exposure to daylight. Judging from the puffy violet shadows around her eyes, Wendy's life is just the opposite.

"Were you trying to nap just now?"

She dips her head and pulls at another hank of hair. "I tried but when I closed my eyes I saw him, on fire. That's not normal, is it?"

Seeing with your ears is a form of occupational synesthesia particular to dispatchers. A cop watches the action in real time, but a dispatcher is left to the cruelty of an active, maybe overactive, imagination.

"You just listened to someone die in terrible pain. That's the part that's not normal. It has to affect you. It would affect anyone."

There's a small tic under her right eye.

"It will take a few days, Wendy, before the memories you have and the sounds you heard stop intruding into your thoughts or your dreams. Not because there's anything wrong with you. It's your mind trying to process what just happened. Talking about it helps. That's why I'm here."

"You want me to talk about the call?"

"If you're ready."

She inhales deeply. Shifts in her chair. Fashions her hair into a loose knot at the base of her neck.

"I was working the shift alone. First, he just wanted to talk. I think he was drunk. Smoking a cigarette. His name is Jerry. He calls 911 all the time when he's drinking. He's on our frequent flyer list. And then he started screaming that he was on fire. I didn't believe him because he says crazy stuff like that when he's drunk. So, I pretended I had dispatched fire and they were on the way, just to see if he'd tell me he was joking. I didn't want to get the firefighters out of bed and then cancel the call. Then I started getting calls from his neighbors. So, I deployed fire for real. I could hear the neighbors banging on his door, but it was locked, and his wheelchair got stuck on something. He couldn't move."

She's breathing rapidly now, her hands pressed against her knees.

"He begged me not to hang up. It felt like hours before the fire engines got there and when they did, they couldn't get the door open either. He was crying. And praying. Screaming for his mother and Jesus and his dog. He didn't want to die alone."

"He didn't die alone, Wendy. You were with him."

"He called here a lot. Sometimes we'd talk for ten minutes. Old people call dispatchers because they're lonely. We're not supposed to tie up the line. But what harm could it do?"

"Sounds like you felt he was almost a friend. That makes hearing him die all the harder."

"I just wish that I had called the fire department quicker. If they had had those extra minutes, the ones I spent talking to him, maybe they could have saved him."

"The truth is we don't know exactly what happened. How the fire started or why it seemed to take so long for the fire department to get there. Could be the minutes you spent talking to him were actually seconds. When you're under stress, your sense of time gets all mixed up. Let's wait for the experts to tell us what happened."

Her shoulders drop slightly. Relief or fatigue, I can't tell. "Is there something I could get for you now, Wendy?"

"I'd really like to go home. It's past the end of my shift."

"Is there someone at home for you to talk to?"

"My parents. And my daughter. My daughter always makes me feel better. Her name is Mysti. She's two, almost three."

"I can give you a few days off work, so you can spend more time with her. Would you like that?"

"Absolutely."

I hand her my business card. "This is my phone number. Call me anytime. If I don't hear from you in a day or two, I'll call you to check in. Is that okay?"

Before she can answer there's a knock on the door, two sharp impatient raps. Wendy jerks back, her startle response in full throttle. I excuse myself and step into the hall, closing the door behind me. Eddie Rimbauer is leaning against his coffee cart, dressed in the only uniform he wears these days: baggy tan pants, a t-shirt, and a stained apron from Fran's coffee shop.

"Heard you were here. It's three o'clock in the morning. You should be at home getting your beauty sleep."

"I might ask you the same."

"I don't need sleep. I'm too beautiful already. Fran has a scanner. Thinks every time there's a crisis, she's got to feed someone." He hesitates. "I'm sleeping in the back of the café. Fixed up a room for myself. Pretty cozy. Money's a little short these days."

Eddie's been sober for well over a year. Still, the demons that drove him to drink are nipping at his heels. The only reason he's had this much leave time is that he had a massive accumulation of unused vacation days. Outside of the local bar, he had no place to visit and no one to travel with. His identity is so tied up with being a cop, that I worry termination raises his risk for suicide. Eddie doesn't have anything else in his life beside work. No friends outside of law enforcement, except for Fran and me, and now, apparently, no place to live. So here he is, almost fifty years old and forty pounds lighter, but not an ounce smarter, hanging around headquarters every chance he gets, still hoping Chief Pence will clear him to go back on duty. The door opens behind me and Wendy looks into the hall. Eddie straightens.

"Good morning to you, young lady. You look like you could use a cup of coffee and something to eat. I have a lovely selection of donuts and sandwiches. Ham and cheese, tuna . . ."

Wendy shakes her head. "No thank you."

"I'm Eddie." He wipes his hand on his apron. "I used to

work in this joint until they gave me the blue juice. Put my ass on leave." He looks at her face, her tired eyes. "You the one dispatched the fire?" She nods.

"Nasty," he says. "You in any trouble?"

"Eddie," I put my hand on his arm. "We need to let Wendy go home. It's been a long night." He shakes my hand off.

"Here's a little free advice, sweetheart. Don't wait to find out if you're in trouble. Get your union rep. And a lawyer. Don't talk to no one. If I learned anything working here for twenty years, it's always wear your vest in the station, because that's where they stab you in the back."

"Eddie!" I'm almost shouting.

"Even if the department doesn't throw you under the bus, the crispy critter in the trailer park may have family and they'll come after you. Not to mention the press. The only person you should talk to is the shrink. She knows how to keep her mouth shut." He winks at me. I wince at his choice of words.

Eddie's faith in me has been hard won and surprises me even now. We started out badly and went from bad to worse in a hurry. Things didn't begin to turn around until his twenty-eight-day rehab. He's been remarkably, actually stupidly, loyal to me ever since.

"Here's the deal, kid. Anytime somebody dies, somebody gets sued. Watch your step."

"Eddie, this is not helpful." Now I'm using my outside voice.

"I'd like to go home now, please. Thanks for everything."

Wendy begins backing away. Eddie unties the strings on his apron. "You're in no shape to drive. Give me a sec. I'll drive you home."

"I'm fine." She keeps moving. "I need my car to take my daughter to preschool. Thank you anyhow." She turns and skitters down the hall.

"That kid needs a friend. She's so scared she wouldn't say crap if she had a mouthful of shit." He watches as she disappears around a corner.

Vulgar as he is, Eddie has that cop ability to read other people—actually, better than he reads himself. Beneath all his bluster, there's a needy boy whose drunken parents let him wander the streets until Fran took him under her wing and kept him there through all the ups and mostly downs of his life. Eddie goes to AA meetings regularly, but every time I suggest he also go to therapy he refuses. Thinks doctors are crooks, in it for the money. He has reason to be suspicious. According to Fran, he spent a fortune on detox clinics and doctors trying to save his wife from the heroin addiction that killed their baby, then her. Eddie has so much unprocessed trauma and grief, it's like he's dancing with ghosts. Hooked by a compulsion to rescue others, he is the one most in need of rescuing.

By the time I get home, the sun is up and so is Frank. He is a remodeling contractor. His workday starts at six o'clock. He hands me a cup of coffee and offers to make me breakfast—eggs, bacon and fried potatoes. I turn him down. I'm too tired to eat.

"So, what's going on at the PD? Why'd they call you in?"

The answer to the question "How was your day?" is never simple for a cop. Or a dispatcher. Or me. Should you tell your family about the maggots on the body you found? What if your wife's hairdresser is married to the local meth dealer? Or your minister is under investigation for collecting child porn? What can I say about talking to a woman who just listened to a man burn to death?

"I don't need a blow-by-blow description. I just want to know how you are."

"I'm exhausted."

"I can see that. What else? C'mon Dot. Nothing is out of bounds. Didn't we agree to share things? Work stuff, personal stuff, whatever."

Frank and I are more than two years into our relationship, living together and planning to get married. Our communication has matured. We don't sit on our feelings. We don't shy from conflict. We regard each other's problems as our own. We have no secrets.

"Yes. No. It depends."

"What does that mean?"

"Yes means we have agreed to share everything. No, means I can't tell you what my clients say because it's confidential. Depends means depends. This was a gruesome incident. I don't want to stick these images in your head. Bad enough I have them in mine. Why should you have to hear about something this awful just when you're about to go to work? It could ruin your whole day."

"Then don't give me the details, just the highlights." And so I do.

2

I grab a few hours of sleep before going back to headquarters. There's a note on my office door. Chief Pence wants to see me. ASAP. Before I have a chance to hang up my coat, he steps into my office dressed in the class-A uniform he reserves for ceremonial occasions and press briefings. He's scowling. Deep crevices mark his forehead and the corners of his mouth.

"I need to vent."

Pence doesn't often take me into his confidence. And he doesn't vent, he dumps. Drops whatever's bothering him in my lap, doesn't take my advice, and refuses to talk about it again.

"I'm meeting this afternoon with the Mateo Park community watch group to discuss the trailer court. We've had this meeting set up for weeks before the fire. According to the watch group, somebody's running a massage parlor out of a double-wide. We shut the damn thing down almost ten years ago. A local crook named Badger was running drugs and hookers. Ask Eddie Rimbauer. He knows all about Badger. He's the reason Badger is in prison.

"After his conviction, Badger went to Frosmer Penitentiary. Maximum security. I thought we were done with him. Now he's transferred to Bradenton, back in the Bay Area to testify in some gang-related case. The guy's as cruel and cagey as they come. Just sits there, fat, dumb and happy, running businesses from his prison cell. It wouldn't surprise me if he had something to do with this fire."

"Runs businesses from his cell? How is that possible?"

"Ever been to Bradenton? Ever been to any prison?" I shake my head no. "Thought so. You should sometime. It's an education. A connected guy like Badger gets whatever he needs—drugs, cell phone access, special privileges. For all I know, he's got half the prison staff on his payroll. All he needs to do is pick up a phone. He gets his gang to do his bidding. Never gets his own hands dirty.

"We raided the massage place twice in the last six months. The first time, the place was locked up tighter than a drum. The second time, there was a family of illegals living there. We scared them to death. They thought we were ICE. Whoever runs the place seems to know when we're coming. Now the hookers are back in business. And with them noise, traffic, condoms, empty liquor bottles, needles." He wrinkles his nose. "The City Council has ordered me to step up enforcement. Form a task force. Shut the place down, once and for all."

He shifts his weight from left to right, as though getting ready to run. "I want Tom Rutgers to head up the task force. He's one of my most pro-active cops. Creative when it comes to catching the bad guys, but not so good when it comes to working with neighborhood watch groups. Thinks citizens should mind their own business and leave catching crooks to the cops. Which of course is idiotic because we need citizen cooperation to find the crooks."

I know Tom Rutgers. He's tall, well-muscled, with dark hair and a moustache. I'll bet women are all over him, something I'm sure his wife doesn't appreciate. Tom has no more insight into his own behavior than Eddie Rimbauer does. On top of that, he's a bully. I saw him intentionally shove a teenage boy into the back seat of a patrol car so roughly the kid cracked his head open on the roof of the car. Tom laughed. Said it was an accident when I called him on it.

"Give me a little help here, Doc. How do I get Tom to lighten up? Change his style?"

Change comes from suffering. Tom Rutgers isn't suffering from anything more than a lack of praise for his proactive style of policing. Being badge heavy has more to do with his ego than any deep-seated psychological distress.

"A person has to be uncomfortable to want to change. Tom seems comfortable with his style of policing. I doubt he's open to changing."

"Dr. Meyerhoff, I'm just asking you to do a little coaching, not commit psychoanalysis."

"What Tom needs is supervision. I'm not qualified to supervise him. For one thing, he wouldn't take direction from me. I'm a civilian. You're the person he'll listen to, especially if you take a special interest in his, for lack of a better term, professional development. As a matter of fact, the more I think about it, the more certain I am that if anyone can get through to him, it would be you."

Pence starts to say something, stops, and walks out of my office without a word. No doubt trying to figure out how his request for my help backfired and why he isn't getting a better return on his investment in me.

3

Pence starts off the Monday morning staff meeting looking crisp and pressed, while the rest of us—a captain, two lieutenants, Raylene, Tom Rutgers and me—are still trying to shake off the weekend. The field services lieutenant begins with the activity report for the weekend: two burglaries, three DUIs, four noise complaints, and somebody's car was keyed, probably by an ex-boyfriend. The Mateo Court neighborhood watch group reported a dark car with tinted windows cruising the neighborhood. By the time the police arrived, the car had disappeared. Pence frowns.

"Extra," he says. "I want extra troops on the street in Mateo Park. I've got Tom here heading up a task force looking at criminal activity in the trailer court. Specifically, the massage parlor."

"What about the fire?" someone asks.

"I have something about the fire." Raylene pushes back from the table and stands. She's wearing a tangerine orange suit, the colorful exception among the muted grays and blues in the room. "I am in the process of investigating our response time. Our standard is to dispatch fire within one minute of receiving the first report. The caller was inebriated and has been known to fabricate emergencies in the past. Our dispatcher spent an additional two minutes talking to the victim, trying to clarify his situation, before deploying fire for a total of three minutes from the time the call was received. When fire arrived at the trailer park, abandoned vehicles and assorted detritus made it virtually impossible for the trucks to get to the fireground. This appears to be a matter of concern for the code enforcement department who may want to bring it up with the resident manager who is supposed to keep the roadways open."

Fire Chief John Clementi opens the door to the conference room. He's a massive man with a deep rumbling baritone voice. The double-breasted brass buttons on the front of his uniform jacket are polished to a high gloss. Gold stripes and stars run up his sleeves like stripes on a barber pole.

"Sorry to bust into your meeting but I know you're waiting to hear from me." He clears his throat and shakes his shoulders like an opera singer preparing to sing a difficult aria. Pence gives him the floor.

"Mobile home fires are complicated. For one thing, mobile homes are built of plastic and compressed wood. Nothing but chemicals. They go up in flames in a second. Even wearing hazmat suits, I was, still am, concerned about exposing my investigators to the toxic debris."

I raise my hand. "What about the people living in the trailer court? Are they in any danger from exposure?"

Pence steps in front of me.

"This is Dr. Dot Meyerhoff, John. You probably haven't met. She's our psychology consultant." He smiles and frowns at the same time. "She asks a lot of questions."

"It's a reasonable question. We do have crime scene tape up and residents have received written notices warning them to stay away. It's a health hazard only when the debris is disturbed."

"Isn't this a magnet for children?" I ask. "Like a big sandbox?"

"The resident manager has agreed to monitor the scene closely."

"We just heard from our communications supervisor that the resident manager's inability to keep the court free from abandoned cars and garbage is what slowed the fire department's response in the first place."

"Your supervisor is correct. Our response time to the entrance of the trailer court was within the standard response of four minutes after being deployed. But, once inside the court, we were impeded by several abandoned vehicles, garbage cans, recycling bins, and so on. We'll look into that, of course. As for the current fire ground, unless Chief Pence is willing to post an officer at the scene twenty-four seven. I'm afraid there is nothing more to be done."

"Enough, Dr. Meyerhoff," Pence says. "Any other questions from anyone else?"

"What caused the fire?" someone asks.

Clementi turns to face the group. "Bottom line. The place reeked of gasoline. The fire started at the front door. Gasoline leaves a distinctive pattern on concrete and those trailers have concrete pads. No question it was deliberately set." There is a collective intake of breath from the group. "Dollars to donuts. You guys like donuts, don't you?" He laughs. So do the cops. Not even a dead man can stop the eternal jousting between cops and firefighters.

"Whoever started the fire, started it near the door with the express purpose of blocking the victim's avenue of escape. Considering that he was confined to a wheelchair, crawling out a window would have been impossible. My investigators also found a partially melted carabiner clamp that was probably used to disable the victim's wheelchair. And the engine ran over a charred gasoline can. Lots of clues for you guys to work with.

Why anyone would want to incinerate a disabled man is above my pay grade. I'm just a dumb firefighter. You have a psychologist on staff. Maybe she can figure it out."

4

"I don't like being home. I'd rather be working. I can't even play with my daughter. Every time she cries or screams it reminds me of Jerry."

"It's only been a few days, Wendy. You're still symptomatic."

We're sitting in my private office. Wendy's wearing a tunic-length black top with cutouts at the shoulders over multi-colored tights. Scorched red blotches mar her smooth pale skin. Her blue eyes are sunk and half-lidded.

"How are you sleeping?"

"Not."

"Bad dreams?"

"Are you going to tell Raylene?"

"All Raylene needs to know is that you've kept your appointments with me. She doesn't need to know what we talk about."

"Somebody told me to make sure this is confidential."

I don't have to ask who that somebody is. The night of the fire, I remember Eddie lecturing Wendy about watching her back. Making himself her guardian. Stepping into his old role as a cop. I need to tell him to stop. To stay away.

"My daughter stays in the room with me. The first night after the fire, she woke me up crying because I was screaming in my sleep, 'run, Mysti, run.' I was dreaming it was her burning alive in the trailer. Scared us both."

"It's pretty common for people to have nightmares after a trauma. The good news is that there are medications with few side effects that can stop them."

Wendy straightens. "I don't like medication. Could I do something natural? Like chamomile tea?"

Cops hate taking medication, even when it would help them. They are afraid of the side effects. Worry it makes them the same as the addicts they see on the job. I wonder why Wendy is so opposed to it.

"I think about the fire all the time. My daughter asks why I'm so grumpy and I snap at her. Tell her to leave me alone. She's only a toddler. I thought I'd feel better being home with her, but I don't. I feel like a bad mother. I'd rather be working. If I was at work, I'd be too busy to think."

"What do you imagine would happen if you went back to work before you were ready and you had to dispatch another fatal fire?"

Her voice drops. "I wouldn't like it."

"It's a possibility though, isn't it?"

"I guess."

"Let me ask it this way. You're telling me—and I appreciate your honesty—that you are edgy, sleep-deprived, and irritable. Would you want to be working with someone who was feeling the same way?"

"No."

"You have PTS—posttraumatic stress injury. It will go away. But you need to be patient with yourself."

"When will it go away?"

"That's hard to say. Generally speaking around two weeks to a month. It depends on a lot of things like how much support you have at home and what else is going on in your life."

"What do you mean what else is going on in my life?"

"If someone has a lot of stress in their personal life, it may take longer to recover from a traumatic incident."

She fiddles with her hair. Bites down on her bottom lip.

"Do you have some stress in your personal life? If you're worried about confidentiality, as I said, this is just between you and me. No one else has to know."

"I'm a single mother. I don't like living with my parents. My mother and I don't get along. She's always trying to tell me how to raise my daughter. That's why I need to go back to work. I want my own apartment. I need a deposit plus first and last month's rent. And I have bills, things I need to buy for Mysti."

"You're on sick leave. You're getting paid."

"But no overtime. I need the extra money." She plays with a small silver ring on her left hand. "I really appreciate you giving me time off, but isn't there something I could do to help myself get back to work sooner?"

"One of the weird things about trauma, Wendy, is that the harder you resist trying to think about what happened to you, the more the memory persists. Confronting it directly is the way to go. Might you be ready to listen to the dispatch tape again?"

The answer to my question comes in a red flush that colors her cheeks and floods the tips of her ears.

"No problem. Let's wait until you're ready. If you're never ready, that's okay too." She slumps in the chair. "I have another idea that might help. Would you be willing to drive out to the trailer court with me? Just to look around. It might help to understand what slowed the fire response. I've taken cops back to the scene of a shooting so they could look around when they weren't fighting for their lives. I know it helped them."

"I don't know. Would you be with me the whole time?"

"Yes."

She closes her eyes, scrunches up her face, and takes a deep inhale as if she's getting ready to jump into a frigid lake.

"I don't want to, not really, but I will. Because Eddie said I should trust you and do whatever you say."

5

The entrance to the Mateo Park Trailer Court is a left-leaning wooden trellis painted white, with the words Welcome to Mateo Park written across the top in faded red. A less welcoming metal sign listing the park rules is set in the ground directly to our right. Residents are to park in designated spaces only, abstain from spitting, loitering, carrying open containers of alcohol, smoking in other than designated places, or making noise after ten p.m. Rule violations will incur fines and possible expulsion from the park. Someone has scrawled "Fornication ok" across the front.

It's a beautiful day, the sun is bright and the skies are clear. On the ride over, Wendy talks non-stop to cover her nervousness. She tells me she lives in Daly City. She only stays with her parents to save money on rent and childcare. They kicked her out of the house when she was pregnant and she only recently moved back. Mysti's father is not involved, never has been. Wendy wants it that way. As for the fire, she hasn't told her parents about it because they wouldn't understand. They think she helps people who call the police when they get locked out of their cars. Or lose their dogs. Her parents are old. She doesn't want to upset them. When they asked why she was not working, she told them she was on mandatory furlough because of budget cutbacks. They didn't press the issue.

The court is a jumble of run-down trailers, parked cheek by jowl, barely two yards between them. It's a miracle that one fire didn't send the entire park up in flames. The narrow streets are strewn with garbage cans and broken-down vehicles. The air smells smoky, tinged with the scent of uncollected garbage. Two lanes converge to our left, forming a triangle. The apex of the triangle is what passes for a children's playground. Hard-packed ground, a worn slide, a wobbly swing set, and a jungle gym so lopsided I doubt it's been played on for years. The base of the triangle is a small swimming pool. Empty except for dead leaves and the torn remainder of an ancient pool cover. Behind it, larger than the others, is a brown trailer with the sign *Resident Manager* hanging from a fluted green fiberglass awning. A webbed lawn chair sits next to the front steps on a square of artificial grass.

"I hope Mysti and I never wind up in a place like this." Wendy says.

I ring the clapper on a large brass bell that hangs next to the screen door. The sound sets off a din of muffled barking. It takes a minute before the door is opened by a woman wearing a purple velour jogging suit and no shoes. She's somewhere between thirty-five and sixty with bottle blonde hair and an inch worth of dark roots. She looks at us over the top of rhinestone-studded reading glasses, her blue eyes moving slowly from my toes to my head.

"No more interviews." I grab the door as she starts to shut it.

"I'm not from the press. My name is Dr. Dot Meyerhoff. I'm with the police department." She raises an over-plucked eyebrow.

"I thought the police were finished here. I already told them what I know." She gives me a second look over. "You don't look like a cop."

"I'm not. I'm a psychologist."

"Oh, for crap sake. I already told the freaking do-gooders from the Red Cross I don't need counseling. I'd take groceries and vouchers for a hotel. I could use a vacation, who wouldn't in this dump?"

"I'm not here to offer counseling. My colleague and I just wanted to look at the scene of the fire."

I turn around, Wendy is ten steps behind me. "She Jerry's family?"

The woman pushes past me without waiting for an answer. "You Jerry's sister?"

Wendy shakes her head. "I'm a 911 dispatcher. I was on the phone with Jerry when he died."

A moment passes, then two as the resident manager takes this in.

"Really?" she says. "Poor baby. Come inside. Let's have a cup of tea or a soda." She looks at me over her shoulder as she opens the door to her trailer. "Some psychologist. Was it your crazy-ass idea to make this poor kid see this up close? After what she's been through?"

She settles Wendy on a flowered couch too big for the cramped space and pushes me toward a plastic stool, proper punishment for my crazy ass ideas. I don't know what to expect next. Maybe poisoned tea. She opens a door at the back of a short hall. An explosion of noise erupts as three rat-sized dogs race into the room and jump on the couch, wiggling and licking.

"They're friendly." The woman shouts out the obvious.

The dogs snuggle close to Wendy. She pats, they lick, she smiles. Pet therapy. Works every time.

"What are their names?" I ask.

"Sammy," the woman says. "All of them. They're litter mates. Hard to tell them apart. Even for me. No point giving them different names. That one there—she points at one with a small notch in its ear—she belonged to Jerry."

Wendy purses her lips and kisses the little dog. "He was calling for you when he died, you know. He loved you." Her voice pitches high, the way people's voices always do when they talk to pets or babies.

"If he loved that dog so much," the woman says, "he could have taken her to the vet every now and then. But he was too cheap. She's only alive because the day before the fire, I got fed up and took her to the vet myself to get her shots. She was a little woozy, so I let her stay overnight with me and the Sammies. Lucky thing I was watching out for her."

"Really?" I say. "On the day before the fire? Wendy, didn't you just say Jerry was calling for her when he died?"

"You can't trust anything that guy said. Bastard lies even when he's on fire."

She hands Wendy and me each a can of soda and finally gets around to introducing herself. Her name is Stell, short for Stella. She's sixty-two and used to be a nurse until the corporations took over her hospital, forcing her to report to some Silicon Valley–style money manager with dollar signs for eyes who didn't know one goddamn thing about nursing. Thought it was all about emptying bedpans and giving enemas. Watched her like a hawk. Timed her, for God's sake, and wrote her up for spending too much time comforting the sick. So, she quit and it wasn't two minutes before they replaced her with some little no-nothing cutie fresh out of nursing school. That's why she's stuck in this dump.

It takes nearly twenty minutes for Stell and Wendy to bond over their love of small dogs, before I remind Wendy why we're here. Stell insists on guiding us to the site of the fire. She drapes a hand-crocheted afghan over Wendy's shoulders and off we go on what feels like a cross-country trek, minus the trail mix. One short street beyond Stell's trailer, a right turn past a slumping camper and we smell it before we see it. Another turn to the left and we are standing in front of an acrid mix of soggy ashes, festooned by yellow crime scene tape. Two white wooden crosses are planted in the ground. A partially deflated mylar balloon tugs against a bouquet of faded plastic flowers tied to one of the crosses.

Stell gives Wendy a hug. "Don't cry over Jerry, honey." As far as I can see, Wendy is dry-eyed. "He was not a nice man. In fact, he was a worthless SOB. I helped him with his catheter sometimes when the public health nurse flaked on him. What does he do? He makes a pass at me, like he's still hot stuff, limp dick and all."

"How long did you know him?" I ask.

Stell turns around as though she's forgotten I'm here.

"He lived here longer than me. Still on two legs when I met him."

"Why was he in a wheelchair?"

"Told everybody he fell down the stairs. If you ask me, more likely somebody threw him down the stairs and then kicked the crap out of him."

Wendy grimaces. "Who would do that?"

"Like I said, honey, Jerry was not a nice guy. He had some bad habits like gambling. My bet is that he owed somebody a lot of money and didn't pay it back."

"Did he tell you that?" I ask.

"Honey, people around here don't talk about themselves. For good reason." She puts her arm around Wendy and gives her a squeeze. "Jerry never paid his rent on time. He tried to borrow money off me. More than once. I told him to pound sand. I worked hard for my money. Loan it to a guy like him? I might as well flush it down the toilet."

"Did he drink?" I ask. "Was he suicidal?"

"Sure. Him and everyone else in this little piece of heaven." Stell fingers the cut end of a piece of crime tape that is flapping in the breeze blowing off the San Francisco Bay. "Why is there crime scene tape still here? When are they going to get rid of this shit? We got normal families living here too, you know."

There's a noise behind us. Officer Pepper Hunt is walking towards us. Hard to miss a six-foot tall woman with spiky fluorescent red hair, shoulders like a linebacker and a voice that would project to the back of the Metropolitan Opera House without a microphone.

"Hey there, what's going on?"

Stell starts to walk away. "I already told you what I know."

Pepper touches Wendy on the arm. She jerks back, like she's been burned. "Hey Doc. Long time, no see." She reaches out to shake my hand.

I've liked this woman from the first time I met her, when I did her pre-employment psych screening for KPD. She was twenty-five then, only two years older than Wendy is now, but way more confident. Spunky. Kind of artsy. Not your typical cop. Dressed like a throwback to the 1960's. Clunky boots, tights, an embroidered peasant blouse under a quilted vest, her hair sprouting like weeds over and under a stretchy headband. Drove all the way from her home in New England to California on a Harley. A world-class swimmer in college, it was only a last-minute shoulder injury that kept her from being in the Olympics. She has a college degree in criminal justice and an honorable discharge from the Army after two years investigating homicides with the military police. All with glowing references. Chief Pence was so thrilled to get a woman applicant with military experience that if I hadn't put my foot down, he would have offered her the job on the spot, no background check, no pre-employment psych. As it was, she sailed through both, prompting a snarky remark from Pence that, not only were his instincts as good as psych testing, they were free.

"Off the property," Stell says over her shoulder. "I'm sick of answering questions."

Pepper raises her hands in surrender. "No problema. I was just out for a walk and I saw the three of you, so I thought I'd stop and say hello."

Stell gives me a "can you believe that shit?" look.

"Doc taking you on a walk-through, Wendy? Good for you. I've done it myself a time or two after a bad incident. Made me feel better to see where things went down. I heard what happened. Rough stuff. Give yourself a little time to get over it." She pats Wendy on the shoulder and this time Wendy doesn't flinch.

Stell turns back, her comforter-in-residence role at risk of being co-opted. "Come on, kid, I'll show you the little dog park I made for the Sammies."

Wendy looks at me, her face one big question mark. I nod my head. The minute they walk away I turn to Pepper.

"Just walking around?"

"Pence has got everybody patrolling Mateo Park. In uniform. In plainclothes. Doesn't matter. I'm thrilled to get off dogwatch. Same crooks. Same revolving door. I need to sink my teeth into something else. I knew this guy, Jerry. I've been out to his place half a dozen times. He was a loudmouth. The kind of petty crook who thinks he's big stuff. Always hanging around, acting like he knows everybody and everything. No visible source of income. I'm thinking he gets money under the table doing something for someone. I've seen him flash a roll, not the kind of money you get if you're on food stamps or disability."

"You think he was involved with the massage parlor?"

"According to the number of women I've seen around his trailer, he's one of their best customers. After all, they're the only ones besides KPD who make house calls."

She nudges a pile of ash with the toe of her Doc Martin boot, then bends down and sifts it through her fingers. A low-slung black car with tinted windows glides by like a prowling shark. Pepper reaches in her pocket for her cell phone. The car shoots off before she can take a photo of the license.

"Badger's boys," she says, half to me, half to herself. "Cruising their territory." She watches until the car turns out of the gate onto the street.

"The chief told me he thinks Badger is running prostitutes from prison."

"So do I. Not just prostitutes. I'll bet he ordered one of his homies to light the match under Jerry's trailer."

"You know Badger too?"

Pepper shakes her head. "Not really. He went to prison before I got to KPD. But he's a legend. All the old-timers know him. Ask Eddie Rimbauer."

Wendy's quiet in the car on the way back to headquarters. "What are you thinking?" I ask.

"Nothing."

"Was this a good idea to come out to the scene?"

"It was okay. I feel sorry for Stell. She seems lonely, like Jerry. All she has are those dogs. She did say a good thing to me. She said being a dispatcher is like being a nurse. Nurses do all the hard work and doctors get all the glory. Same for dispatchers and cops. Made me feel good to hear her say that."

"Cops are brave. Wendy. But listening to Jerry die showed you have a kind of courage few people have."

"Stell said he was a bad person. Maybe he was. I didn't want him to die like that. I didn't want him to die at all. Except when I couldn't stand his screaming anymore. What kind of a person does that make me?"

"You didn't want him to die, Wendy, you just wanted his agony to stop. Both your agonies. That's very different than wishing a person dead."

"Is it?" She shoves up against the passenger side door and doesn't say another word.

6

Tom Rutgers watches as I pull into the parking lot to let Wendy out at her car. He opens the back door and waves me into the building. Walks a few yards to the coffee room, looks inside and motions for me to follow.

"Dispatcher having a meltdown? What's she got to complain about? She wasn't at the fire. She didn't see it, didn't smell it. Dispatchers read the book; cops get to see the movie."

I want to tell him that you don't have to have a gun in your face to be traumatized; it's enough to be exposed to the horrific details of someone else's ordeal. Instead, I ask him what he wants.

"You know the chief has appointed me to run Operation Happy Endings." He watches to see if I know what he means by happy endings. I do. "When it comes to shutting down massage parlors, I'm his man."

"Your point is?"

"The chief told me to talk to you. He thinks I'm a little rough around the edges. I have too many citizen's complaints. That's because people whine when you throw them in jail. I'm Pence's best cop. His top performer. My stats are better than anyone's. That's why he's appointed me to run this operation. That place should have been shut down for good a long time ago." He leans forward, loosens his grip on the doorknob. The vending machine rumbles. "Just so you know, this community policing shit is nothing but a feel-good publicity stunt. Making nice with the community is the chief's job, not mine." He opens the door. "So, just in case the chief asks, let's consider this little confab all the coaching I need. You okay with that?" Before I have a chance to answer, he wishes me a nice day and walks down the hall.

Typical Pence. Asks my opinion and then ignores it. I told him I wouldn't counsel Tom and he tells Tom I will. Now, thanks to his manipulations, Tom's got the upper hand. He's turned me into his confederate: the two of us against the chief. I don't like it and I'm sure it's not going to end well.

7

Frank has dinner waiting when I get home. Grilled shrimp with honey mustard sauce and a salad.

"Call your mother. She wants to come down this weekend and take you to Nordstrom's to buy a wedding dress. Fine with me except I won't be around on Saturday. My photo class is spending the day taking pictures in San Francisco."

"Shopping? The wedding's not until spring. I don't know why she wants to make such a big deal out of this."

"Because getting married *is* a big deal. Tell you what, if you wear a wedding dress, I'll wear socks." He kisses me on the cheek and dances off into the kitchen.

The last time I shopped for a wedding dress was over twenty years ago. Back then my mother thought weddings were an unnecessary extravagance. "What's important is what comes after the wedding," she said. "Spend your money on furniture or food. Not on some frou-frou dress you'll never wear again." She waved a tailored navy suit, straight skirt, fitted jacket, in front of me. "Very smart. Very basic. You'll get a lot of wear out of this. A little hat, a bouquet, and you'll look like a blushing bride."

My parents didn't much care for my first husband, Mark. My father had nothing good to say about most people in positions of authority, but he had special animosity for academics after he'd been kicked out of Berkeley. He was caught on tape, not for the first time, giving the finger to the local cops, his pockets full of rocks. Considering the beating he got after his arrest, expulsion wasn't the worst of his punishments.

Mark and I married in city hall, our two sets of parents as witnesses. The ceremony, if you can call it that, was wedged between more important things. Mark was under deadline for his next book. The semester was ending. He had dissertations to sign off. The few photographs I kept show the ceremony was as grim as it was quick. Mark looks nervous, not just because he was getting married, but because he was marrying me, his graduate student, a not uncommon joining that was nevertheless looked upon with courteous disdain by the older, risk-averse, administration.

I look nervous because I can feel the tension wafting around us. My father, standing off to the side, looks disgruntled. He should have been happy we didn't get married in Mark's parents' church. He hated religion in most of its forms despite being fiercely and paradoxically loyal to his Jewish roots. Mark's parents look dour. Marriage wasn't legal unless God was involved. The only one who looks at all happy is my mother who was overjoyed because we'd saved money, avoided falling prey to the avaricious wedding industry and were about to celebrate our good fortune by eating Chinese.

My mother calls again after her sit and stretch class to discuss our shopping trip.

"Mom, I'm not wearing a white wedding gown. I'm fifty-three years old and, shocking as it may seem, I'm not a virgin."

"Don't talk to me like I'm old and don't know what's happening. I want you to have a special day. Whoop it up. Your first wedding was so ," she hesitates, "funereal."

"Do you remember why? We didn't have a big beautiful wedding because you, Mother, thought it was wasteful. That Mark and I could do better things with our money."

In an era of alternative facts, my mother is a star. Either that or her memory is failing at an alarming speed. My father worked his entire life in a small print shop he didn't own. What else does a man with one good arm and a hatred for anything remotely corporate do for a living? If it wasn't for my mother's efforts to revise reality into a rosy scenario, what she called living lightly off the land would have been seen for what it really was; living within shouting distance of poverty. The fact that my mother now lives comfortably on next to nothing in a lovely senior citizens community is due to the largesse of a very rich family, probably oil barons or scions of the military-industrial complex. They underwrite her rent because she is, in their diplomatic terms, income eligible. The only thing my father made sure of was that we lived so purely, so free of corporate contamination, that we wound up broke.

"Not me. Us. Your father and me. The bride's family is supposed to pay for the wedding. Your father worked too hard to throw his money away on something that would last an hour. Maybe less. Capitalism exploits people, persuades them to want things they falsely believe will make them happy. Your father and I resisted this kind of thing all our lives."

This is what my mother always does. Turns poverty into a noble cause. Twists things around until she finds a happy narrative she can live with.

"So why now, Mom? Why a big wedding and a white dress?"

"It's your second marriage. You're paying for it. I'm not."

8

Raylene stops at the door to my headquarters office the next morning. We're on our way to meet with the chief. At his request. Raylene is a swirl of green and purple like a tropical bird floating in a sea of midnight blue. Every day, another colorful outfit, an antidote to working in a dimly lit basement room with blinking monitors and no outside windows. She pushes the button on the elevator.

"How did it go yesterday?"

I tell her about Stell and what she said about the victim. "Wendy's still struggling with survivor's guilt. I hope it was some small consolation to learn that Jerry wasn't a boy scout."

"Coffee, ladies?" Pence pushes up from his desk as soon as he sees us in the doorway. He gestures at three small chairs surrounding a cheap wooden table holding a coffee pot and a stack of cobalt blue mugs embossed in gold with the KPD insignia. Car lights from the outside streak across the bay window behind his desk, creating tread marks across Raylene's face. She releases a long breath, soft as a run in a nylon stocking. "So, Doc, how's our dispatcher doing? If it would help, I'm available to give her my usual pep talk. How being able to laugh at the stuff we see in this crazy business is as important as carrying a gun."

That's my line. Pence has a nasty habit of appropriating my advice as his own, using it at the wrong time with the wrong people and bristling with annoyance whenever I point this out to him.

"That would be helpful," I say. "Except, as you know, dispatchers don't carry guns."

"Let's get down to business, shall we? Raylene, I've called you and Dr. Meyerhoff to my office because the other day, when Chief Clementi made his report, you used the term 'enhanced call' to refer to the victim's status. I didn't have time to ask. What is an enhanced call?"

If Pence paid any attention to the 911 dispatchers, he should know what an enhanced call is. But he doesn't, because dispatchers aren't cops, they're civilians and most of them are women. All of which adds up to second-class citizenship in his department.

Raylene clears her throat. "Eighty percent of our calls for service are from mentally ill citizens. Or about them. Sometimes, people are so desperate they will tell the dispatcher whatever they think will make the officers get there sooner. Many of our enhanced calls come from the Mateo Park Trailer Court. There are a number of mentally ill people housed there for lack of other available shelter."

"Our dead guy was mentally ill?"

"We have had several enhanced calls from the victim over the past few months. He gets drunk, reports someone is breaking into his trailer trying to kill him. Other times, he wants to kill himself. Most often, what he really wants is to talk. Or a ride to the hospital to get his medications refilled. He could be having a psychotic episode or he could be drunk. Our dispatchers aren't trained to tell the difference."

Raylene has asked for training many times since I've been

here. Pence always refuses. Training means overtime, travel expenses, extra money, begging the City Council for funds. The priorities in his training budget always go to the cops. But now, facing possible inquiries about the death of a wheelchair-bound man, not to mention the bad press that's already started, I suspect he's about to have a change of heart.

Pence shakes his head. "Nut job. Was he ever armed?"

"The burn victim? I don't believe so. Other residents of the park? Frequently."

Pence's eyebrows lift, as though he was hearing this bit of news for the first time. He rotates in his chair until he and I are face-to-face. "Dr. Meyerhoff, this is a dangerous situation. I don't want any of my officers killed or injured because dispatch didn't or couldn't assess the situation accurately, including a determination about the presence of weapons on scene. I would like you to give the dispatchers some training in dealing with the mentally ill."

Typical Pence, ignore a problem for months or years and then go for a solution Code 3, lights blaring, sirens on.

"Sorry, but the mentally ill are not my area of expertise. It's an ethical violation to operate beyond the boundaries of my competence." This is the second time in recent days Pence has asked me to do something and I've refused.

"Be that as it may." Raylene's voice coils around the tension between Pence and me like a silk ribbon. "I would be grateful for whatever you have to offer us, Doctor. You may not believe you know enough about mental illness, but I can assure you, whatever knowledge you do have exceeds anything my dispatchers have."

I know very little about dealing with psychotic people. I spent one summer as an undergraduate working at Miller State

Hospital for the Insane, later renamed The Miller Psychiatric Institute to sever any association with padded cells, forced lobotomies, and convulsive shock therapy. Call it what you will, it was still a hell hole for people so crazy or violent they didn't respond to the miraculous anti-psychotic drugs of the 1950s.

Forced to do community service in grad school, I volunteered in a crumbling SRO hotel, repurposed as a homeless shelter. The place filled to bursting every night as staff scrambled to plug holes in the VA system for returning vets, crazy from drugs and PTSD. I felt like we were—to use that mangled but apt metaphor—rearranging deck chairs on the Titanic. Futilely trying to manage the tidal wave of homelessness that started after draconian budget cuts shut down the state mental hospitals, releasing thousands of mentally disturbed patients to the care of nonexistent community programs. I'm not without pity for these poor souls. I wouldn't want to be terrified of things others can't see, tormented by voices no one else can hear. But I didn't have what it takes to deal with the stink and the shouting. And the violence.

I met my ex-husband, Mark, in grad school, right after I completed my internship at the shelter. I was exhausted and demoralized. Wondering why I was spending all this time, money and energy on grad school to wind up in a five-story fleabag hotel treating untreatable clients with auditory hallucinations and oozing skin disorders. I had been looking forward to a cushy practice full of YAVIS—young, affluent, verbal, intelligent, and successful clients. Or an ivy-covered life in academia, writing books and teaching eager students who hung on my every word.

Mark was teaching an experimental course in police psychology. Titled something like "Helping First Responders Help Themselves." I was attracted to him and to the topic.

Working in the homeless shelter, I had daily contact with cops, often several times a shift. Ninety-nine percent of them handled our drunk and disorderly residents with respect and restraint.

This was a different generation of cops from the cops that beat my father, but the job was still the same. Show up and help people who would just as soon lie to you, give you the finger, throw-up in your patrol car, or give you a case of scabies. I saw cops go out of their way for homeless families, the working poor with salaries so low they couldn't pay the rent or the doctor. Hand a hungry man a five-dollar bill to get a sandwich, knowing that the five dollars wouldn't be spent on food. Comfort a runaway who'd been selling himself on the street, then come back three or four times to check on the boy's whereabouts and find him a foster home.

Police psychology was new, unexplored territory. I didn't share my father's hatred for law enforcement, despite the fact that beating him sentenced my mother and me to years of listening to his rants and scraping by on his next-to-nothing salary. He was provocative. They were over the top. It happened a long time ago.

"Good, then that's settled," Pence stands. So does Raylene. "Take whatever time you need to get competent, Doctor. Just don't take too long."

"Do you have another minute, Chief? I'd like to talk to you about Tom Rutgers."

Raylene gives me a look and hustles out the door. Pence looks surprised. I never discuss my clients with him.

"We had a short meeting yesterday. Counseling him is not going to work. He lacks the necessary insight or motivation."

Pence's face mashes into his customary what-do-I-pay-you-for look.

"He's apparently a good cop. You seem to have a lot of faith in him, so my best recommendation is to stay close to him. Like I said, if he's going to accept feedback on his tactics from anyone it would have to be you. I'm just a civilian."

Pence puffs up with the implied compliment.

"I could order him to see you. Would that help?"

"Please don't do that. He'd do it, but only because it's an order." Authority and power, the feel of the boot on his neck, is the only thing Tom Rutgers respects. "If you make seeing me mandatory, it will make him more defensive. And my job harder."

"I have a lot of faith in Tom. The arson fire and the massage parlor activity are likely connected through Badger, the incarcerated criminal I told you about the other day. For this reason, I'm considering combining the homicide and the massage parlor operation investigations into one and having Tom run the whole thing. Your thoughts?"

Pence rarely asks for my opinion before he takes action. More commonly he makes a decision and then asks what I think.

"Handling two major cases at once, even though they may be connected. That's a tall order for one person, Chief. And a lot of media exposure."

Pence dives into his own thoughts, as if he hasn't considered that an investigation of this magnitude would place his pet cop in front of the media on a daily basis.

"How about partnering Tom with Pepper Hunt? When I took Wendy to visit the trailer court, Pepper was doing extra patrol at your direction, interviewing witnesses and so on. She's been working midnights for a long time and is looking for something different to do. She impresses me as mature. Articulate. Has good people skills. If I remember right, you were eager to hire her because she worked homicide when she was an MP. This is a high-profile case. KPD has had a reputation for sexism. Having a female at the front of this investigation is evidence that your efforts to bring more women on board are working."

Pence turns his chair toward the window behind his desk, staring out at the parking lot, like a cat fixated in front of a gopher hole. I continue talking to the back of his head.

"Tom can share the limelight or be out of it entirely. Less stress for him and the more time he'll have to focus on the investigation."

Maybe I'm selling this too hard, but there's a kernel of truth in what I'm saying. As egotistical as he is, Tom prefers the accolades of his peers to the questions of an impertinent and skeptical press.

Pence spins back in his chair to face me. "Good call, Dr. Meyerhoff. Good call. I'm going to give her serious consideration."

Serious consideration from Pence is usually a "yes." He stands. We shake hands. For the moment, things between us feel a little more balanced and a little less tense.

9

"Gracias, arigatou, merci, and danke. The chief called and asked me to coordinate with Tom Rutgers on the Mateo Court gig. Said it was your idea. I'm really stoked. Sit down, please. Lunch is on me."

Pepper is in the back booth at Fran's, the one Fran usually saves for VIPS. With a flourish, as though he's delivering pheasant under glass, Eddie sets a menu on the table in front of me along with my usual glass of iced tea. He recites today's specials, recommends the hot turkey sandwich and when I tell him I'm not hungry, he just stands there, hoping we'll ask him to join us. When we don't, he backs away from the table, bobbing up and down like a servant. Being a police outsider is crushing him. The only way he knows how to cover his hurt is to mock himself.

"So," I say. "Did I do the right thing recommending you to the chief?"

"Absolutely. Like I told you, I'm going down the tubes on midnights." She raises her iced tea in a toast to me. "Thank you, thank you. I can't say it enough."

"How are you going to like working with Tom Rutgers?"

"Don't know. Never worked with him. The guys on my squad

love him. Think he's a cop's cop. He doesn't mince words, I'll say that. Told me he likes working with women because they're better at kissing ass with the public."

"He really said that?"

"Cop humor. You got to roll with it or this job will kill you. Especially if you're a woman." She shovels a forkful of salad in her mouth like she hasn't eaten in a week. "I want to talk about our victim, Jerry. Here's how I like to think about a murder case. First, I start with the victim. From my previous contacts with him, my guess is that Jerry was some low-level functionary for the gang that runs the massage parlor. He ticked somebody off, stole some money or some dope and they killed him.

"Secondly, I like to think about the killer's motivation. In this case, they were probably trying to send a message to the rest of the flunkies. Step out of line, this is what happens. Terrorism on a local scale." She slathers butter over a roll, bites into it. chews hard, and puts half of it back on the plate. "Tom thinks tactically, not psychologically. That's why I wanted to talk to you. Hope that's okay."

It's plenty okay with me. Pence is the one who won't like it. He's forever warning me to stay out of criminal investigations and stick to counseling cops. Frank won't like it either. He worries I'm going to get hurt or killed. Or get him hurt or killed when he tries to protect me. Pepper finishes off the roll, wipes her buttered fingers on a napkin.

"I'm curious, Doc. What was your take on the park manager, Stell?"

"She's certainly got a grudge against the world."

"My thoughts exactly. She's a junkyard dog, protecting her territory. Her bark's worse than her bite. She doesn't like cops so we can't expect a lot of cooperation. But I don't put her in the frame."

"Ladies?" Eddie's back with a coffee pot in one hand and a pitcher of iced tea in the other. "Refills?" He starts pouring tea into my nearly full glass. The overflow puddles on the table. "Back in a minute with a rag." He leaves the pot and the pitcher behind.

"The famous Eddie Rimbauer," Pepper says. "He's got a jacket for being a very good cop and an even better drunk."

Eddie swoops back in with his cleaning rag and attacks the table like he's cleaning up a crime scene, then fakes exhaustion and plops down into the seat next to me. Pepper introduces herself.

"I heard about you," Eddie says. "Heard you and pretty boy Rutgers are heading up the Mateo Court investigation."

It never fails to amaze me how quickly news circulates when cops are involved.

"I'm on leave at the moment, but I'm available for consultation. Just saying. Any day, any time. Don't hesitate. I live in back of the café. Temporarily, that is." He gives me a look. "I know the Mateo Trailer Court. Once a cesspool, always a cesspool. A guy named Badger used to run the joint. A real scum bag."

"Eddie," Fran calls from the kitchen. "I don't pay you to talk to the customers."

"You don't pay me at all, you slave driver." He starts to scramble out of the seat and Pepper stops him.

"Wait a minute. Tell me about Badger." He slides back in, making a show of still wiping the table.

"You're asking the right guy. I'm a proctology detector, board-certified finder of assholes. Badger's a bad, bad dude. He's got a rap sheet as long as my arm. Spent more time in jail than out. Starting when he was a kid. Usual story. Father in prison, mother working the streets, foster homes, in and out of juvenile hall. Worked his way up to prison by running girls, dope, and killing off the competition. He's a worthless piece of shit. Short, squat, ugly as sin. Thanks to me, he's also got a helluva limp. One of my proudest moments was sending that bag of shit off to prison for the rest of his life." Pepper is scribbling notes in a small notebook. "He's doing time at Frosmer where only the tough survive. Courtesy of yours truly."

"No, he's not," I say. "The chief told me he was transferred to Bradenton, back in the Bay Area."

Eddie's face goes white. "No fucking way."

"Eddie." Fran's voice sails through the air like a frisbee "I'm not asking twice."

He scrambles out of his seat, takes two steps toward the kitchen and turns back to Pepper. "Write this down in your little book. Don't make no never mind that I'm on leave. If Badger's involved, I still got a dog in this hunt."

As soon as Eddie is out of earshot, Pepper slaps her notebook closed. "This is my lucky day. Badger's transfer to Bradenton saves me a trip to Southern Cal. I think I'll breeze up there tomorrow. Meet the infamous Badger in person. Although, to tell the truth, I probably know all I need to know. You only have to look at his rap sheet. I've met hundreds like him. They're all the same."

I want to ask how she can be so sure. Was I that filled with certainty at her age? Or is she buoying herself up to take on the biggest, most important, most frightening, assignment of her young career?

"Okay, Doc. I need to get moving. I got lots to do."

"Can I go with you?" I say.

"Back to headquarters?"

"To Bradenton. I've never been inside a prison. Just yesterday, the chief told me I should visit one. I'm a little embarrassed that

I never have. It's part of every cop's work life. I should have more firsthand knowledge."

"Happy to have you along. For the company and for your input. You've just done me a big favor getting me appointed to the task force. I'm happy to have a chance to return it." She slides out of the booth. "Tomorrow morning. seven o'clock sharp. Just one thing. When we meet with Badger, I do all the talking."

10

I meet Pepper in the police garage. The sky is mottled gray and threatening rain. Frank insisted I take his battered metal coffee thermos because he wants me wide awake, given my plan to spend the morning in a walled city of thieves and murderers.

Pepper is chugging from a water flask. We head north on 280 past the rolling coastal mountains and the tree-shrouded Crystal Springs reservoir. Fog drapes over the hills like a giant wave. Pepper dodges in and out of traffic, fearless in the knowledge that if she's stopped for speeding, professional courtesy means it's unlikely she'll get a ticket. She's a master at multitasking, talking and driving like she's in a high-speed pursuit. As soon as we approach Nineteenth Avenue in San Francisco, the traffic slows, but not Pepper. Her fingers tap the steering wheel, her eyes darting left to right, looking for an opening to pull forward. She strains against the enforced pace, making funny little whistling noises between her teeth.

"I did more research on Badger last night," she says. "His real name is Bunny. Bunny Bollard. His mother named him. Thought his ears were too big and he looked like a rabbit. He picked the name Badger himself because badgers are short legged, nocturnal, and capable of fighting off enemies bigger than they are. Like Eddie said, he's got a rap sheet as long as my arm, starting when he was thirteen. Also, thanks to Eddie, he has a helluva limp and extended stay status in prison at the taxpayer's expense."

Pepper hits the horn at the car in front of us, punishing the driver for making us wait an excruciating three extra seconds to drive forward after the light turned green. The driver returns the favor with a single-fingered wave. Now we're speeding again, crossing the Golden Gate Bridge. Alcatraz to my right, the Pacific Ocean to my left.

A double decker tourist bus pulls next to us, the top deck crammed with shivering people. Tourists are always surprised at how cold the Bay Area can be. And equally surprised to find the world-famous, mile-wide bridge isn't gold, but international orange. The name Golden Gate comes from the narrow strait that runs beneath the bridge, separating San Francisco Bay from the Pacific Ocean. It was christened in 1846 by Army Captain John C. Fremont as the "Golden gate to trade with the Orient." I learned this from Frank. Being in construction, he loves bridges. And tunnels. And buildings of all shapes and sizes.

Another twenty minutes and we are in the Bradenton parking lot. The prison looms over us, massive and medieval. Frank would be fascinated. A guard reads the visitors' instructions aloud: no colors that might be confused with the blue denim worn by inmates, no military green like the guards, no jewelry, no purses, no food, no cigarettes, no phones, no wigs, no camouflage, no photos with sexual or gang-related images. Definitely no weapons. I sign a release of liability declaring that I am entering the prison on my own accord and, in the event of my untimely death by an inmate or by officers attempting to restore order, the prison is not liable or responsible. Should I be taken hostage, I should not expect to be saved or traded for a prisoner's release. In the event of a blaring siren I should remain standing while the inmates sit down, unless gunfire erupts at which point, as though I am devoid of basic survival instincts, I am instructed to "hit the deck."

Pepper has dashed off her signature and is tapping her foot, eager to get going. The guard collects our waivers and matches us and the other visitors with our photo IDs. Pepper marches ahead. I follow behind, trying to convince myself that prison uprisings happen more often in warmer weather. There's another back-up at the main entrance as we wait to be "wanded" for hidden metals and hand-stamped with an invisible mark. The invisible mark is needed so the guards will know who to let out in the unlikely event that some self-sacrificing visitor has switched identities with a prisoner.

Pepper stiffens the minute we get past the main entrance. "I put some of these guys in here. They may not be happy to see me." Her fingers search for the gun she was required to lock in the trunk of her car. Guns are forbidden. Even the correctional officers don't carry them for fear of being overpowered by an inmate and taken hostage.

A tall, muscular correctional officer walks us to the administrative segregation unit for maximum security prisoners. He laughs as he instructs us, just in case we need it, on the art of dodging packets of urine and feces. Pepper's wearing jeans, a sweatshirt, and a puffy down vest. I feel like a fool wearing my just-back-from-the-cleaners suit and a silk shirt.

The interview room is small, stuffy, and evil smelling. The walls are institutional green, with smudges of something black or brown. A metal table sits in the middle of the room clamped to the floor with huge bolts. There are three chairs, two on one side of the table, and two doors, each one with a screened window. In all four corners, a video camera hangs from the ceiling.

I hear him before I see him. Hear his shuffling feet, the clinking sound of his shackles and handcuffs. A correctional officer opens the door and steps inside. Looks around the room. His eyes pass us, like we're no more interesting than the chairs we're sitting on. Badger enters next, followed by a second guard who closes the door behind him.

Badger is huge: world-class Olympic-level, weight-lifting huge. And, like his namesake, short, built close to the ground and limping like a ship rocking at sea. Every bit of his skin is covered in tattoos. He shuffles towards the single chair like a mythological creature—half man, half Persian rug—and gives us the once over.

"I'm pushing forty, but when I asked you guys to get me a woman," he says to the correctional officers, one at each shoulder like human epaulets, "I didn't mean Grandma Moses and an Amazon. This the best you can do?"

Pepper flashes her badge. Badger looks at it out of half-closed eyes.

"KPD? My favorite police agency. Is my friend Eddie, the old booze hound still around? I'd love for him to visit so I can show him what shooting me in the ass did to my hip. Lousy fucking shot. Should have killed me on the spot."

"I'll be sure to give him the message," Pepper says.

"So, ladies. What can I do you for?"

Pepper explains that she's investigating the death of a man named Jerry who lived at the Mateo Park Trailer Court

"Jerry? That the dude that got french fried? Never heard of him."

"Then how'd you know he got french fried?"

Badger looks at her. Something between a smile and a smirk crosses his face. "It was on the radio. The education channel."

He looks at me and winks, his eyes nearly hidden in the swirl of markings inked on his face.

"Listen Red, I don't mean to be rude, but, if, perchance, I had any information you could use, what do I get in exchange?"

"I have nothing to bargain with unless you have something to give." Pepper is leaning against the back of her chair, tipping it on two legs, her arms folded over her chest.

"So, what do you want to hear?"

"Let's start with who told you about Jerry?"

"I have devoted followers, they're like pen pals. They send me all the neighborhood news."

"Why was Jerry killed?"

"Who said he was killed? I heard he smoked himself. For real." He laughs. "That was a joke, Red. Smoked himself. Got it?" He turns to the officers. "Fucking cops, no sense of humor."

"How well did you know him?"

"He's a creepy little guy. Didn't know how to be a friend. Pay back a favor. You know, quid pro quo."

"What favor?"

"That I didn't kick his ass out on the street when he flaked on the rent."

"That's it?"

"That's it. It's a thing I have. I don't like people who welch on their debts."

"Did he work for you? Is that how he was supposed to pay you back?"

"I asked him to suck my dick. He declined." Badger tries to reach his crotch for illustration but can't because of his handcuffs.

"He was in a wheelchair, any idea how he got there?"

Badger shrugs again. "Maybe tripped over his shoelaces?"

"Do you still run the massage business?"

"Me? I'm locked up lady. How am I going to run a business?"

"You have subordinates."

"I don't got subordinates. I got hemorrhoids."

"Do you know a woman named Stell Martin?"

"Is she good-looking?" Pepper doesn't respond. "Never met the lady."

He turns to me. Studies my face. Slowly. Deliberately. I can feel his eyes crawling over every pore.

"What's with you, lady? Cat got your tongue?"

"My name is Dr. Dot Meyerhoff. I'm a psychologist. I work with KPD." Pepper glares at me. I've just broken her only requirement to let her do the talking.

"I already got a diagnosis. I'm a sociopath with psychotic features and anger management issues. Plus, my mommy didn't love me." The correction guys are trying hard to suppress smiles. Badger wields a certain vulgar charisma that must get him special treatment from the staff. "Like I said, I might be more help if you had something interesting to offer. I don't give stuff away for nothing." He's talking to Pepper, but still looking at me. I feel like a bug under glass.

"What do you want?" Pepper asks.

"Two hours a day in the yard. And ten thousand dollars to donate to our libtard governor in the hopes that Governor bleeding-heart follows up on his campaign promise to end over-crowding and release a bunch of us for good behavior. I'm already the beneficiary of his progressive ideas. Bradenton beats Frosmer by a mile, even in ag seg." He winks at the COs. "I'm going to get out of here someday, Red and I'll need money. Strictly legit. I have an heir."

"I don't exchange money for information."

"You got kids, Doc?"

I start to respond. Pepper touches me on the arm, motions me to lean in. "He's baiting you. Don't give him any personal information. Leave this to me." She pushes me away. "Tell me about the massage parlor."

"You want to talk about massage parlors? My favorite legit business, unless the Republicans have made healing hands illegal while I've been in the joint." He laughs. Checks my reaction. "Is there a specific massage parlor you want to talk about?"

"The one you run. The one in the Mateo Park Trailer Court."

"Used to, I told you. I got out of that business years ago. Hard to run a business long distance. Didn't even know it was still open."

"You have connections. No doubt you have a cell phone. You could run the United Nations from here if you wanted to."

"All my connections are criminals. If I let them run my business, if I had a business, they'd be skimming off the top. Better I just use my time here to improve myself." He looks at me again. "Do I know you from somewhere?"

"Hey," Pepper slaps her hand on the table. "Me. Talk to me. Not her."

"You got kids, Red?"

"We've been setting up on the massage parlor in Mateo Court for weeks. Every time we get ready to bust the place, everything's closed up tight. Nothing but nuns inside. Would you know anything about who might be giving the ladies a heads up?"

"No kids, huh. I'm guessing you don't like men."

"That's it, we're out of here." Pepper pushes out of her chair. The metal legs scrape over the floor.

"Hold on," Badger says. "I have a question for the doc."

"Not going to happen." Pepper opens the door to the hall and gestures for me to get up. She's bristling with command presence. Badger is watching the two of us. "Don't answer. He's after something."

I turn my back to Badger, lower my voice to a whisper. "We've been here thirty minutes and he hasn't told you anything worth knowing. Let's play bad cop, good doc. See where it takes us. What harm can it do?"

She purses her mouth. Scowls and lets go of the door. Badger doesn't move. We walk back to the table. Pepper takes a long breath and opens her palms in my direction like some flunky sidekick introducing the star of the show.

"What was your question?" I ask.

"Where did you work before KPD?"

"I had a private practice."

"And before that?"

"I was in graduate school. Why?"

"Ever work at the Kenilworth homeless shelter?"

"Where is this going?" Pepper looks annoyed.

"Not to worry Red, me and the Doc are taking a little trip down memory lane. Sorry if you feel left out."

Pepper's hands ball tight.

"I did. I had an internship there while I was in grad school. I was there for about a year."

Badger smiles. His teeth are blackened in places, missing in others. "You don't remember me, do you? Of course, I was younger, had hair, no tats, and no limp. I was an angry little shit, living on the streets, selling myself."

A memory pokes at me. Vague, dim, cloudy.

"I bounced in and out of the shelter a few times until some goody two shoes cop found me what he said was my forever home. All the guys thought you were hot. You didn't have no gray hair then. It was you that got that cop to get me a foster home, wasn't it?"

I remember him now, a skinny little kid with a wide smile. Clowning, joking, desperate for attention.

"That's it." Pepper opens the door to the hall. "Reunion time is over. We're leaving. Now." She holds the door and waits for me to exit first.

"Nice to see you again, Doc," Badger calls out. "Let's stay in touch."

Pepper is silent on the way home. Not a mutter at the traffic clogging the freeway. The only sound I hear is the clink of her teeth as she saws her jaw back and forth.

"That's how you get TMJD."

"What?"

"Temporal mandibular joint dysfunction. You know, from grinding your teeth. Clenching your jaw."

"This was a freaking waste of time."

"Not for me. Blows my mind he remembered me. It was so long ago."

"How come you didn't remember him?"

"I do now. I can't believe how much he's changed. He was so small. Way smaller than other kids his age. And funny looking."

"That hasn't changed."

"We all felt for him. He looked like a child and he was selling himself on the street. And smart. Lots of potential."

"He's not small anymore. Short, but not small."

"I think he's clinically depressed. Did you hear him say he wished Eddie had killed him?"

Pepper slouches against the driver's seat, small muscle tics vibrating under her jaw.

"People like Badger don't have feelings. Be careful, Doc. He'd say anything to get your sympathy." She leans on the horn, all her agitation aimed at the sea of red brake lights in front of us.

I think of Badger as a kid. How he made us laugh. How he was so smart the staff all thought he might be that one-in-a-hundred shelter resident who would make it in the world. What happened to him between then and now to turn him into the man I just met? Sadness settles on me. We are all changed by time, some for the better, others for the worse.

"What's with you, Doc?" Pepper says into my silence. "Feeling bad about Badger? Listen to me," she says. "Compassion doesn't work with guys like this. I know his type. Take my advice. He's playing you, thinks you're a mark. If he contacts you for any reason, I don't care what it is, let me know. ASAP. Don't go near him and whatever happens, don't do anything he asks."

11

Dr. Philipp—with three p's—Rogoff's psychology office is on the first floor of a brick mansion that has been converted from a spacious family home into a complex of medical offices. I made an appointment with him last year and cancelled it. At the time, I was having fears about getting married, fears that when Frank got to know me he'd be disappointed and leave me for another woman like my ex did. But I've grown to trust that Frank loves me as much as he says he does. Things are strong between us. We have a date and a place for our wedding. Iowa in the spring when the corn and tomatoes are ready. I'm excited. He's excited. It's just that, as the date gets closer, I'm having a minor attack of cold feet. A temporary setback. A little bump in the road. I can take care of it, once and for all, in one, maybe two sessions.

Frank thinks cold feet are normal. That I'm worried about nothing. He says getting married in our fifties has a lot of advantages. We skipped the hard parts. No money worries, no children to raise, our careers are settled, and our ambitions quieted. We know who we are and have accepted the futility of trying to change our partners. On the other hand, being as old as we are means we're realists. We know what lies in front of us.

"Not today, not tomorrow, not even next year, but someday,"

Frank said as he walked me to the door after dinner, “I won’t always be this good looking, so it’s best you work out any lingering doubts about your ability to tolerate me when I’m fat and bald.” Then he started whistling the Beatles song *When I’m Sixty-four*. “To think,” he said, “Paul McCartney wrote that when he was sixteen. I was never that smart when I was a kid. But I am now.” He kisses my cheek. “I know a good woman when I see one.”

The real Dr. Rogoff bears little resemblance to the photos of the eager, energetic Dr. Rogoff on his website. He’s much older. There are streaks of gray in his brown hair and his spine curves slightly, stooping his shoulders into a perpetual hunch, as though, despite the degrees on his wall, the world is still a puzzle to him.

Dr. Rogoff specializes in relationships because, as he says in a colored block of text on his homepage, situated next to a split image of two trees, one barren and one in bloom, “I know, first-hand, the pain of heartbreak and the joy of healing.” I found this both reassuring and off-putting. Yet, here I am.

My psychology training was strictly tabula rasa, blank slate, give nothing away. If a client asked me a personal question, I’d bounce it back, query why they were asking, what it meant and what they’d do with the information if I chose to answer. I was trained to remain neutral. Go for the transference. Be a stand-in for someone else.

When a client projected his feelings for his boss onto me or mixed me up with her withholding, cold-as-ice mother, I was to acknowledge and interpret these unconscious mistakes, because this was what was making my client miserable. Didn’t matter if my client was idealizing me or knocking me down. It was all grist for the mill of self-understanding.

Dr. Rogoff doesn't specialize in self-understanding, he specializes in problem solving, coaching, and actionable advice for getting on with life. "Fix the problem, not the blame" is his brand. It's on his business cards, his stationery, and the brass plaque outside the front door to his office. He promises not to waste time going back in time. If we don't solve the problem in four sessions, he'll offer a fifth at no cost. And he doesn't take insurance.

Four sessions sound like more than I need and I'm relieved not to review my childhood once again. All graduate psychology students have therapy before they graduate. How else will they know how it feels to sit on the other side of the desk. And I'm happy to pay in cash so I don't leave a record. That would be all Pence and the entire staff of KPD would need to hear. If our department psychologist can't handle her own problems, how can she help us with ours? It's a fair question. But it makes me feel like a hypocrite. I try to encourage cops to get therapy, normalize it as the healthy, responsible thing to do if you have a problem. And here I am hiding my own.

First on my list of things to talk about are these annoying fears that keep popping up out of nowhere. I know how shrinks think. If Rogoff knows his stuff, despite his promise not to go back in time, he'll ask me about my first marriage, and then, I-know-it's-coming, my father.

I decide to beat him to the punch. Before he asks, I tell him how I turned a blind eye to Mark's infidelity in the same way my mother turned a blind eye to our poverty and my father's eccentricities. On the one hand, I knew Mark was unfaithful. On the other hand, I didn't want to know. I ignored all the signs. His lack of interest in sex. All the psychology conferences he attended without me. "Costs too much if we both go," he said when I asked to go along. "One of us has to stay home, cover our practice and handle emergencies." Now I know why that one of us was always me.

Mark said he didn't want children, not until our practice stabilized financially. Then he left me for Melinda and had a child with her. Now, of course, it's too late. At fifty-two, Mother Nature has taken the decision out of my hands.

"So," Dr. Rogoff says after I finish talking, "your father was a self-involved narcissist with delusions of grandeur, in denial about his true station in life, and your ex-husband lied to you about his affairs, his desire to have children, and ultimately left you for a younger woman with whom he has since started a family."

"That about sums it up," I say.

"I'm curious, how is it that you followed in your ex-husband's footsteps, choosing to specialize in police psychology?"

"I never mentioned his specialty. Do you know him?"

"Mark Edison? Certainly. Doesn't everybody? He has an expert opinion on everything from murder to politics and is very good at generating publicity for himself on the evening news. Strikes me as a fabulous phony with situational ethics. He's a very obvious narcissist, like your father."

Rogoff waits for my reaction. His bloodhound eyes topped with gray-flecked, wiry eyebrows. I notice for the first time that he needs a haircut and a dandruff shampoo. Not only that, his leather furniture reeks and he's left the price tag on the silk ficus next to his desk.

"So now, you have found a decent man, one who declares he loves you and actually backs this up by treating you with respect. A man who appears to have his own life in order, no neuroses, no bad habits. He wants to marry you. Spend the rest of your lives together. But you, faced with love and decency, suddenly develop cold feet. How do you explain this?"

I don't like this line of questioning, even if I predicted it. When I don't respond, Rogoff opens a drawer in his desk. Removes a pair of reading glasses, a small bottle of glass cleaner and a folded cloth. With the concentration of a neurosurgeon, he sprays each lens on both sides, wipes the glass dry, refolds the cloth and puts both back in the drawer. It's a delaying tactic. He's insulted me and is trying to figure out how to repair the damage. More than an answer, he wants to make certain I don't give him a bad rating on Yelp.

"So," he says finally, breaking the silence, "our time is nearly up. I leave you with this question to contemplate until our next session. Why, with the kind of history you have with men, would you trust me, a male, to be your therapist?"

12

KPD sits in the middle of Silicon Valley. Once filled with orchards, there are now as many artisanal coffee shops as there were fruit trees. It's a beautiful afternoon, unseasonably warm. The sun bounces sharply off an angular glass building and falls gently on the renovated Spanish-style mansion next door. Kenilworth is the county seat. The population is exploding like everywhere else in Silicon Valley. Office buildings are moving into old, gracious, tree-lined neighborhoods. Restaurants are elbowing out retail stores that have served the community for decades, only to fold in a month and be replaced by another one-of-a-kind eatery. The deep-throated clang of a pile driver shakes the shop windows—another new building to decorate the landscape, each one taller than the last, turning this once low-slung bedroom community into a high-rise haven for start-ups and venture capitalists.

Instead of my office, I've arranged to meet Wendy on the vine-covered patio of Kenilworth's newest Italian café, designed to look as though it's been there since Columbus discovered America. The tatted and pierced barista with half-blue, half-black hair is only too eager to make our coffee drinks. Her eyes, lined like Cleopatra's, follow as I look at the swirl of cream on top of her foamy creations and take my first sip. I give her a thumbs-up and she breaks into a smile, revealing a metal stud in her tongue.

Wendy looks better than she did a few days ago when we visited the trailer court. More rested. More color in her face. She's wearing a flounced skirt and a jersey top with cutouts at the shoulders. She smiles as she thanks me for the coffee. I notice something I have missed. Dimples, big, deep, charming Shirley Temple-sized crevices that light up her face.

"How are you doing, Wendy?"

"Better."

"Sleeping?"

"Better. A lot better."

"Any bad dreams?" She shakes her head. "None?"

"Just one. A really short one. Woke me up. I went right back to sleep though. I think I'm ready to go back to work. It's fun being with Mysti so much, but. . . ." She stops herself, eager to tell me how much she wants to return to work, but cautious about sounding like a bad mother. "Any more news about the fire?" she asks.

"Nothing you don't already know." I count on my fingers. "One, someone intentionally set the fire; that's why the trailer burned so fast. Two, the fire department was slowed down by debris in the trailer court. Three, there was absolutely nothing you could have done to change the outcome. Talking those extra two minutes did not contribute to his death." I pat her hand. She gives me a weak smile, as though what I just said was not the slightest bit consoling.

"Hey there." Pepper's voice sails in over my shoulder. She pulls up a chair and sits, uninvited, cell phone in one hand, a large latte in the other. Pepper is a good cop, she's smart. She's certainly motivated. Energetic to the max. Still, I'm beginning to wonder if she isn't also over-caffeinated, hyper-vigilant, and untrusting. What gives her the right to follow me like I'm a suspect?

"C'mon Doc, I know what you're thinking. I'm not trailing you. This is my favorite coffee shop. Fran's behind the times. People want espresso drinks, cappuccinos, not percolated coffee. Don't tell Eddie I jumped ship." She winks at me. "How you doing, Wendy? You look better. Feel better?" Wendy nods. Pepper gives her a soft punch to the arm. "Good girl, because I got a favor I need to ask."

Pepper motions us forward, drops her head, inviting us to do the same, like co-conspirators.

"Remember Stell from the trailer court? Remember she mentioned Jerry had a sister? I'm trying to get a good victim profile of Jerry. I'm thinking the sister could give me some information, only I don't know her name or where she lives. There's nothing in the public records. Stell's not fond of cops and not inclined to help me out. You seemed to get along well with Stell. So, I was thinking, if you asked, she just might give us the sister's address. Would you do that for me? Talk to Stell?"

Wendy looks at me. Questions written all over her face. Pepper's request is out of the blue and highly improper. She's asking a recently traumatized woman to expose herself to possible re-traumatization. She should have talked to me about this before she put Wendy on the spot. Wendy is vulnerable on two fronts. She'd do anything to get a clean bill of health and go back to work. My intuition also tells me she doesn't have very good boundaries which generally means, when someone asks for a favor, she has a hard time saying no.

"Maybe we should talk about it first, Wendy. In private. Give you some time to think it over."

"That would be great, *if* we had the time." Pepper is talking to Wendy and looking at me. "Cases like this, time is of the essence. We don't want anyone else killed, do we?"

What a guilt trip. I resist the urge to kick Pepper under the table. I'm wearing open-toed shoes. I'd probably break my toe. My wedding is only months away. I don't want to risk walking down the aisle wearing an orthopedic boot.

"I could do it this afternoon. My mother's watching Mysti." She looks at me. "If I do it, can I go back to work?"

"This is not a trade-off, Wendy. Or a test. Pepper can get the information she needs some other way if she has to. Helping solve a murder is not your responsibility."

Pepper looks at me like I've just poured salt into her latte. "But I want to do it," Wendy says to me. "If I can help it would make me feel better. As long as you come too."

13

Police cars are noisy and hot. And in this case, dirty and littered with empty coffee cups and food wrappers from last night's shift. Pepper mumbles something about slobs under her breath as she sweeps the mess into a trash can. "Should be a law," I say.

"There is. General orders. All shifts are responsible for cleaning up their cruisers. Everybody knows it. Not everybody follows." She turns to me and Wendy. "So, Doc, do you mind taking the back seat? I think Wendy would be more comfortable in the front."

She opens the rear door, swipes the bench with a paper towel and guides me to the back seat, as though I were under arrest, placing her hand on my head so I don't hit the door jamb. Wendy scoots into the front. She's never ridden in a police car before. A ride-along should have been part of her training. I make a mental note to tell Raylene. Pepper gets behind the wheel. The big engine rumbles loudly.

"Buckle your seat belt, Doc. If I hit a pothole, you're going to bounce."

I buckle up and look around. There are no handles, the back door opens only from the outside. The bench seat is made of hard black plastic, no crevices to hide weapons or drugs. A big metal screen separates me from the front of the car making it hard to hear or see.

"Okay back there?"

"Fine," I say. "Just peachy."

Stell is waiting for us outside her mobile home, dressed for company in a pink velour jogging suit, bejeweled gold sandals and earrings that dangle and glint in the sun. She gives Wendy a big smile and marches her into the house. Pepper and I follow. The Sammies are frantic with joy, alternately racing around the room and jumping on Wendy as if she was covered in hot dogs. Stell gives Wendy an appraising look.

"You look better, how are you feeling?"

"Better. A lot better."

Pepper takes a small notebook out of her pocket. "Thanks for agreeing to see us."

Stell whips around, the tag ends of her hair sticking to her lipstick. She swipes her hand over her mouth. "I'm only talking to Wendy. Not you." She looks, or rather glares, at me. "Not her neither."

"Please, Stell," Wendy says. "They're trying to help. Someone murdered Jerry. It's a homicide investigation now."

Stell is stoic, unreadable. As though Jerry being murdered is not news.

"If Pepper knew more about Jerry, that might help her find who killed him."

Stell coughs out a laugh. "Knock on every door. You'll find a hundred people here who wanted to kill him. I told you before. He was not a nice man. He had a run-in with every goddamn person in this park."

"Officer Hunt wants to know how to find Jerry's sister. Even if Jerry was the worst person in the world, he didn't deserve to die like he did. It was horrible. I know. I listened to him die." Her face reddens and her eyes fill with tears. "Please help her find Jerry's sister. It would help me too."

Stell starts digging in an enormous green purse. Pepper and I look at each other. Either Stell's more of a pushover than we expected or Wendy's better at the art of persuasion than either one of us had imagined. When she doesn't find what she's looking for, Stell throws her purse on a chair and starts shuffling through a pile of newspapers on the kitchen counter until she finds a paper address book with a missing cover. She flips through the pages, finds what she's looking for, copies it down on a piece of paper and hands it to Wendy.

"This is the last address I had. I'm only doing this for you, because of what you went through. Be sure to tell your cop friend here to keep Jerry's gold-digging bitch of a sister off my back. She thinks Jerry had a fortune hidden somewhere. I told her, if it was in his trailer, it went up in smoke. He was still months behind in the rent."

Wendy's quiet in the car on the way back to HQ, unmoved by our praise for how quickly she got Stell to give up Jerry's sister's address.

"She's lonely, like Jerry was. I'm good with lonely people. All she has are the Sammies. Not the same as having friends. Or a husband to come home to."

I know she's talking about Stell, but I wonder if she isn't also talking about herself.

14

The aroma of mushrooms, tomatoes, and cheese mixed with a spicy-sweet fragrance makes my stomach growl the minute I walk through the front door. A large glass vase filled with red and orange roses sits on the dining table. It's not my birthday. Not Valentine's Day. No one's died. It's just the plain Jane middle of the week. Frank walks out of the kitchen wearing a denim apron, a glass of wine in each hand. We kiss and clink glasses.

"Thank you for the flowers, they're beautiful. What's the occasion?"

He kisses me again. "Beats me. Ask the person who sent them."

"You didn't send them?" He shakes his head.

"They were sitting on the front step when I got home. In a plain brown box."

There's a card taped to the vase. It's homemade out of old cardboard, the edges rough and torn in places. The writer pressed hard with his pencil, leaving indentations, like reverse Braille.

Dear Doc: No lie. I have a son. Please help me find *him. I'm desperate. Badger.*

I hand the card to Frank.

"Is this from the guy you went to visit yesterday in Bradenton prison? Why is he sending you flowers?"

I remember Pepper's warning. That Badger was playing me. Thinks I'm a mark. If I hear from him, I should tell her and not do anything he asks.

"He remembered me from when I was interning at a homeless shelter while I was in grad school. Said I was nice to him."

"Now he wants you to find his son? I don't get it."

"He did mention that he had an heir. We didn't think much of it. He said a lot of things and wasn't very cooperative."

"But why you?"

"I don't know, I can only guess. I'm trying to put myself in his place. How would I feel if I just met someone from my long ago past, someone who knew me before I turned into the person I am today? Someone who might remember something good about me. Who might be willing to help me again, if I could show them that the good side of myself was still here, buried under a ton of muscle and ink for protection."

"Sounds like the plot for a Grade B movie."

"He was an appealing child, desperate to be liked, but smart, with a really quirky sense of humor."

"And now he's a convicted criminal who knows where we live. I tolerate a lot from your job Dot, but I told you a long time ago, my tolerance ends when your work puts us in danger."

15

Pepper is waiting for me at headquarters, leaning against the wall outside my office, a giant paper cup of coffee from the Italian coffee shop in each hand and a crinkly sack stuffed in the pocket of her quilted vest. I open the door; she kicks it shut behind her, sets the coffee on my desk and tears open the paper bag. Four biscotti, each one drizzled with chocolate.

"You're supposed to dip those in coffee to soften them," I say as she bites down on a dry biscotti. "What's up?"

"I met Jerry's sister Shayla last night. She lives right where Stell said she did, over by the ocean. She's a primary school teacher, moonbeam, hippie type. Decorates with seashells. Says Jerry was dyslexic, always in trouble, started drinking when he was a kid. Never had steady work. Did pick-up jobs here and there. No training, no skills, he just did stuff for other people.

"Her husband runs a small marina and rents fishing boats, sets lobster pots, repairs engines, that kind of thing. He invited Jerry to go in with him, offered to teach him how to fix things, do maintenance. Jerry would be enthusiastic for a week or two and then stop showing up for work. Shayla didn't think Jerry could read the instruction manuals."

"Did she say how he wound up in a wheelchair?"

"Told her husband he got drunk and fell down a flight of stairs. She isn't sure she believes him."

"Girlfriends?"

"The sister thinks if he wanted female companionship, he had to pay for it. I asked her where he got that kind of money. She didn't know that either. Said whenever he had a little extra, he didn't hang on to it for long. No mention of a hidden fortune, like Stell said. Sometimes he would brag about having money, but he lied to everyone, including himself." Pepper finishes the last of her coffee. Pitches it into the wastebasket with perfect aim.

"She didn't seem too upset when I told her we were investigating his death as a murder. Said, and I quote, 'Whether he killed himself or somebody else did it for him, dying young was in the cards. Jerry's always been a loser. No matter what kind of hand he got, he was bound to lose.'"

The whole time Pepper's talking I'm debating about telling her about the flowers and the note from Badger. If I don't tell and she finds out, which she's bound to—Frank threatened to call her if I didn't—that would be worse.

"I have something to tell you. Badger sent me flowers and a note. They came to my house last night."

Pepper sits up in the chair, her face gone hard and blotchy. "I need the box, the flowers, the vase, the note. I want everything fingerprinted."

"I don't have them. Frank threw everything in the garbage. With my permission. The garbage was collected this morning."

"Damn it. I should never have taken you with me."

"You didn't take me. I asked to go. You only said yes."

"What does he want?"

"He asked me to help him find his son. Remember he said he had an heir?"

"He said a lot of shit." She stands. "Next time you hear from him or one of his homies, you call me immediately. I don't care what time of the day or night. I warned you he was going to play you. He's a bad seed. Always was. Always will be."

"I take it you don't believe in rehabilitation, that, given the right circumstances, people can change."

"Listen to me, Doc. Or ask Eddie Rimbauer. You can't rehabilitate a person who was never habilitated in the first place."

16

"Did I do okay? Did Pepper talk to Jerry's sister?' Wendy bombards me with questions before I can open the door to my private office. "Can I go back to work now?"

"Slow down, please. I need a minute to get organized."

She starts pacing. I can feel her following me with her eyes as I hang my coat on the hook behind the door, loop my purse over the back of a chair and open my briefcase.

"Tea? Coffee? It will just take a minute."

"No thanks."

"Mind if I get a cup?"

"It's just that my Mom's waiting for me in the car with Mysti. Mysti cries when I leave her. She's probably driving my mother crazy."

"Are you sure you want to go back to work? I can give you more time off."

"Mysti's gotten too used to me being at home. Before, when I worked nights, she'd be sleeping when I left and just waking up when I got home. Now that I'm there all the time, she screams whenever I leave the room. I feel like I'm in prison."

"You can invite your mother and Mysti inside. There are toys and a sand box in the waiting room. I have a colleague who treats children."

"I don't need a session. I just want to know when I can go back to work."

"You were very helpful with Stell and yes, Pepper talked to Jerry's sister."

"What did she say about Jerry?"

"Not much. They weren't close. Still sleeping okay? No nightmares?"

She shakes her head. She does look better than she did even a few days ago. The bags and shadows under her eyes have receded and there's color in her face.

"I've been walking every day like you said. I take Mysti to the park. We feed the ducks. She loves ducks. I decorated her whole room with ducks. Duck wallpaper, duck sheets, lamps that look like ducks. At the pond, she talks to them, but then she's afraid at the same time. Throws food and runs away when they come for it. Makes me laugh."

"A couple of weeks ago I told you that when you go back to work, there's a high probability you'll have to dispatch another fire, maybe even a fatal fire. Do you feel ready?"

"Yes, I think so. I think I'm ready."

"Think? Not certain?"

Her cheeks flush. I take this as a sign to move slowly. Once she goes back on shift, there will inevitably be triggers, reminders of Jerry's death that will provoke a reaction.

"Before we decide on a date for you to return to work, let's do this. I'm going to give the dispatchers a full day's training about handling emotionally disturbed callers. The idea for the training came up after your incident because Jerry was an emotionally disturbed caller. Come to the training. It will give you an opportunity to see how you feel being back at work. If you feel okay, then we can talk with Raylene about a date for your return, maybe start you off with half a shift at a time."

"Every day I'm out, means another dispatcher has to pull an overtime shift. They take hard calls too, all the time. I don't want people to think I'm getting special treatment."

"If you had broken your leg, everybody would understand. They would manage without you. Psychological injuries may be invisible, but they are just as real and hurt just as much. Everybody you work with knows how awful that call was. I don't think anyone resents you taking the time off."

She stops pacing, pulls at a clump of hair.

"Is there something else you're not telling me Wendy? You seem almost desperate to return to work."

"I told you. I need money and I need to get away from my mother. I feel like I'm in prison. It's either her or Mysti. They're always watching me. I can't get a minute to myself."

Someone leans on a car horn.

"See what I mean?" Wendy gestures toward the window. "That's her honking the horn."

As soon as Wendy leaves, I make myself an overdue cup of coffee and settle in to work on my teaching plan for the dispatchers. My cell phone vibrates, skittering toward the edge of my desk. I know who it is, the minute I hear his voice.

"Hey Doc. You gotta help me. I'm gonna' die in this place. I got money saved for my boy. Lots of. . . ."

The phone goes dead. My hands are shaking. I tell myself to calm down, consider my options. Take a deep breath. I should call Pepper, that's the first thing I should do. But I'm afraid she'll go ballistic, charge up to Bradenton, demand Badger be transferred back to Frosmer and make solving Jerry's murder all the harder. Then she'll warn the entire KPD police force never to take me into their confidence when it comes to investigations because I am a liability, a bleeding-heart liberal who wouldn't know a crook if he sat in my lap.

The second thing I should do is tell Frank. What if Badger calls me at home? But if I tell Frank, he'll drive right over to headquarters and demand that Pence give us protection. Then Pence will go bonkers and fire me for interfering with police business, totally ignoring the fact that he was the one who told me I needed to visit a prison in the first place. I take another deep breath. I'm catastrophizing. My amygdala is on fire. I'm too agitated to think clearly. If I do anything it will probably be a mistake, so, for the time being, I decide to keep Badger's telephone call to myself. The man's locked up, what harm can he do?

17

The communications center at KPD is on A-level, steps from my office at headquarters. A dimly lit room without windows, it's where the 911 dispatchers sit leashed to their consoles for ten, twelve hours at a time, their faces illuminated by the light from a circle of flat screen monitors. Once again, Raylene is the only spot of color in a bright purple suit with silver studded purple nails to match. She stands as soon as she sees me and starts to gather a stack of papers, moving with the grace of a woman half her size and half her age.

"Upstairs please. Your training is in the conference room. Fran's up there now, putting out fruit and pastries. She'll be back in the afternoon with lunch."

"How did you pull that off? Last I heard about budget cuts, the city isn't paying for anything but coffee."

"I have my ways," she says. And I know, without being told, that she's picking up the tab herself.

Eddie is wearing a clean apron and a collared shirt. He pushes the coffee cart to the conference room wall and plugs in a giant metal samovar. As soon as he bends down Fran waves me over to where she is arranging food.

"Eddie has a crush," she says loud enough to be heard. "On a dispatcher."

He stands up. "And you are a dirty-minded old witch. She's a kid, needs a little help, she's not interested in a fat old bastard like me."

"I hope that's the case," I say, knowing Eddie is compelled to find needy women to rescue—first his drunken mother, then his addicted wife. Freud called it a repetition compulsion. I call it a disaster about to happen.

Eddie opens an ice chest and digs around for milk and juice. "What's with you women anyhow? I'm old enough to be her father."

The door to the conference room opens and dispatchers begin to file in. Raylene stands at the door, part hostess, part mother, inviting everyone to help themselves to food. This is her chance to offer something to KPD's civilian stepchildren. Something concrete to show them how much they matter, if not to the cops or the community, to her.

Eddie fusses with the food, his eyes searching the room. He doesn't stop until Wendy rushes in, out of breath, no make-up, her hair wet and stringy.

I have at least four months' worth of training to deliver in four hours, minus the hourly break. I lose ten minutes just waiting for Wendy to settle in. Every dispatcher in the room wants to give her a hug, tell her how much they missed her. I start by reading the agenda with a short explanation for each item.

- Recognizing the signs, symptoms, and thoughts of persons in crisis.
- Recognizing various types of emotional disturbance

(psychoses, substance abuse, PTSD, panic, depression, etc.) and appropriate responses to each.

- Assess and manage an individual's risk for suicide.
- Active listening techniques to verify information, de-escalate, and defuse.
- Understand the dispatcher's role in officer safety and improving field contacts with callers by developing triage questions to determine if there is a mentally ill person on scene, if that person is in or out of compliance with medication, has a mental history, a treating doctor, or a gun.
- The cost of caring: Developing self-care skills for your own physical and emotional well-being; dealing with cumulative stress, acute stress, PTSD, secondary trauma, and compassion fatigue.

The last item is the one I feel best qualified to teach. I look around the class. Wendy's head is down, studying the handout.

After the training, Raylene and I sit together as Eddie and Fran pack up the leftover food. I'm exhausted, my throat is sore from talking. All I want is a glass of wine followed by a nap. Neither of which I can get at headquarters. Raylene is eager to have Wendy back at work as soon as I think it's safe for Wendy and for the public. Back filling for Wendy and another dispatcher who is recovering from surgery is putting a strain on her staff and her overtime budget.

"She still seems a little shaky. There will be another emergency, another fire, I can't guarantee how she'll react."

"I'm not asking for any guarantees, Dot. I've been at this long enough to know there aren't any. Everybody reacts differently to different things at different times. What used to bother me, doesn't bother me anymore. On the other hand, stuff that used to roll off my back can make me crazy.

Let's give Wendy a chance, see how she does. Start her back slowly, maybe half a shift, day after tomorrow? If she does well, I'll give her another half shift. If that goes well, I'll put her back on the schedule full time. I'm burning out my other dispatchers. They don't complain, but I can feel it. Not to worry, I'll keep my eye on her."

18

"And you cancelled your appointment last week because. . . ."

"I can't remember. I was busy. We have an active homicide investigation."

Dr. Rogoff's head tilts like a day-old tulip. "Please, Dr. Meyerhoff, I am a professional therapist. When you left here two weeks ago, I asked you a question you have yet to answer. I believe that is why you missed last week."

"Can you repeat the question, please?"

He looks at his notes. "Why, with the kind of history you have with men, would you trust me? Or better yet, pretend to do so."

"Now I remember. Sorry. We therapists are bad clients, aren't we?"

"What I'm saying is that you haven't yet decided to be a client, you're merely visiting, checking out the goods. Just as you're doing with your man friend. Always an escape valve close at hand."

This is only my second session and he's flinging interpretations at me. "Building trust doesn't happen overnight. You know that as well as I do. It is my responsibility as a consumer of therapy to check you out. And it's your responsibility to earn my trust."

"Dr. Meyerhoff, you looked at my website before you made your first appointment, did you not?" I nod. "What conclusions did you draw?" He doesn't wait for an answer. "My guess would be that after perusing my website you found me to be slick, superficial and therefore harmless. Someone you could manipulate, who would just skim the surface.

"I don't have the time to work with visitors, only declared clients. And I don't have the patience to prove myself trustworthy to someone who can't trust. It's not me you need to trust, Dr. Meyerhoff. It's yourself."

"How do you suggest I do that?"

"Ah yes. You'd like a recipe, a formula." He looks beleaguered. "All my clients do. Alfred Adler promoted the as-if principle back in the 1920s, or in today's parlance, 'fake it 'til you make it.' I prefer the Adlerian version." He looks at me. "Sounds simple, doesn't it? Perhaps a bit shallow? But then again, isn't that why you chose me?"

19

Two weeks pass without any further contact from Badger. Jerry's murder and the massage parlor investigation are stalled. I start to relax. Badger's moved on to something else. Or someone else. I was right, Pepper was wrong. I'm not a mark and Badger's not the devil incarnate.

"Earth to doctor." Pepper is standing in my open office door watching me read my email. "Tom and his team raided the massage parlor again last night. Without telling me, I might add. Guess what happened. A big, fat, nothing. Zip. Zero. Zilch." She illustrates by making zero signs with the thumbs and index fingers of both hands. "Nobody home except one very grouchy hooker in a pair of oversized flannel PJs. They woke her majesty up and she wasn't happy. The team looked all over the double wide and didn't find so much as a condom or a smoking doobie. Tom's been watching the place. He knows there's at least four girls working every shift."

"I don't understand."

"It's obvious, we got a leak. I told Tom weeks ago we need a CI, someone on the inside. Know what he said? He can't sell it to the chief because confidential informants cost money and they're not reliable. Guess what? I marched into the chief's office, told him we needed a CI to move things along and I knew one who would be perfect. He said yes. Didn't blink an eye."

Pence has his favorites. All depends on who is doing what to make him look better.

"Tom thinks he's Supercop, but when it comes to asking the chief for something, he turns into a spineless wonder. I told Pence funerals cost money too. Badger's minions are all over the place. Next time they know we're coming, instead of a woman, there might be a guy with a gun." A small muscle starts pumping across her forehead. She folds her arms over her down vest and grins. "I hate waiting around for things to happen. Next time there's a raid, I want to be out in front of the game."

"How did Tom react when you told him the chief said yes to the CI?"

"He mumbled something under his breath. Probably for the best that I couldn't hear it. The massage parlor and Jerry's murder are linked. I'm one hundred percent certain. All I'm doing is lighting a little fire under Tom's butt. Moving things along because nothing's happening for either of us. Not unless Badger's tried to contact you again."

My stomach lands somewhere south of my knees. I turn away from Pepper, open a file drawer, put some handouts in a folder and slam the drawer shut. Giving myself just enough time to let the heat out of my face.

"Tell me about your CI. Who is she? Where does she come from?"

"I bought her online." She looks at the expression on my face. "Just kidding, Doc. It's a quid pro quo thing. Some women are willing to cooperate in the interest of working off a petty charge, shop lifting, drug possession. Some of them have kids. They don't want to go to jail."

"So, your CI is a woman with children?" Pepper shakes her head.

"Pixie's a kid, just shy of twenty-two. When I was working mids I picked her up for shoplifting. Third offense. She was facing jail time. Typical story. Father sexually abused her for years. Pimps her out to his friends. She finally tells her mother. Mother doesn't believe her. Slaps her around. She runs away. Lives on the street. Starts hooking, stripping to pay the rent. I found a little weed on her, told her I'd forget about it and the shoplifting if she'd work for me. She jumped at it. She's actually pretty good. Smart. Catches on quick. Might have been a decent cop if she didn't have a record. You'd like her."

20

The window behind Pence's desk is opaque with unexpected rain. Pence has called Tom and Pepper into his office for an update on the investigation before he leaves for the day. Pepper requested I come along to offer some psychological insight on Stell or Badger. I think she just wants an ally. Pence doesn't ask me to leave, but he doesn't look happy that I'm there.

He asks the first question without looking up from his notes. Silver reading glasses that match his hair glint on the end of his nose. "Just to be sure I'm clear on this, you don't think the sister, Shayla, had anything to do with her brother's death."

Pepper nods in agreement. Tom says he never rejects a potential suspect until the case is closed and the guilty party is in jail. He's wearing a sport jacket and tie for the occasion. Pepper is Pepper, same outfit, different colors.

Pence turns to Pepper. "What's the report on your CI?"

"AOK. She's staying in regular contact. Glad to be off the street. Out-calls, in-calls, a little low-level dealing. Happy endings guaranteed."

"Why aren't we shutting this place down?" I ask, violating my intention to sit quietly unless someone asks me a question.

"Because Dr. Meyerhoff"—Pence talks slowly, exaggerating

each word—"the massage parlor is still part of an ongoing homicide investigation. On the scale of criminal conduct, homicide trumps prostitution." He turns back to Pepper. "Please continue."

"My CI has been asking around about Jerry. As we thought, he was a customer. Did some minor stuff in exchange for services. Used to be the bag man until he got hurt. Not much you can do from a wheelchair."

"Guess the girls had to give him a hand," Tom says. He laughs and looks at Pence for male-to-male reinforcement. Doesn't get any and sinks back in his chair. "I just hope your CI knows what she's doing. CIs lie a lot."

"I know Pixie. She's reliable. Not yours to worry about." Pepper shifts in her chair so her back is turned completely away from Tom. She's stone-faced, her fists shoved deep into the pockets of her vest. Pairing her up with Tom doesn't seem to be working.

"Here's what's happening on my end," Pence counts off, finger by finger. I can't tell if he's oblivious to the tension in the room or deliberately avoiding it. "The mayor's climbing up my ass. The Mateo Park Neighborhood Watch is climbing up my ass, followed by The Mateo Park Community Board, the Mateo Park elementary PTA, and the Mateo Park Council of Churches. If I have any more evening meetings my wife's going to leave me. Half the groups want to shut the trailer court down. Trash the place and build a park. The other half wants to keep it open, get rid of the hookers and turn the place into respectable low-income housing."

"Who owns the park?" I ask, violating my intention to be quiet for the second time. Pence does not look happy with me.

"A shell company. One of those phony off-shore deals, no offices, no employees, no owners."

"I talked to the resident manager, a woman named Stell." Tom says. "Twice after you two talked to her. She's a piece of work. Doesn't know anything about anything, including who pays her salary. Says it comes on a bank check. So long as it cashes, she doesn't know from nothing. I'll tell you what she does care about." He stops for effect. "Wendy, our dainty dispatcher. Both times I was there, so was Wendy. Making cookies, playing with the puppies."

Pepper and I look at each other.

"I told Ms. High and Mighty manager, it's her job to keep the trailer court up to code. Get rid of the garbage and the clutter. Part of the reason our vic is dead, is because the fire trucks couldn't get through the street. That's a criminal offense. Unless the mystery landlord is indemnifying her, she's looking at jail time."

Pepper's face mottles with color. "You tried to get a material witness to cooperate with our investigation by threatening her with criminal prosecution and jail?"

"Making nice with her hasn't gotten you anywhere, has it? I was just ratcheting up the pressure. She acts like this is a joke. Jerry was a loser. Who cares if he burnt himself up?"

"So, how did that work?" I ask.

"She told me to get my butt out of her face and slammed the door."

Pepper and I drop by the comm center to check with Raylene. Wendy is doing well, back to her old self. She starts her shift in an hour, but as usual, she's in early. We find her in the locker room, rolling her hair with a curling iron. There's a radio playing and she's dancing a little as she twists long bands of hair into loose spirals that cascade to her shoulders. She greets me with a smile until Pepper follows me in.

"You look happy," I say.

"I am. I am so happy to be back at work. Mysti's adjusting, getting used to having me back on my old schedule."

"We just came from a meeting with Chief Pence and Tom Rutgers. Tom mentioned he saw you at Stell's place. Twice."

She turns the volume down on the radio. "Am I in trouble?"

"No way," Pepper says. "We were just curious about what you were doing there."

Wendy unplugs the curling iron. Lays it on the counter. "I went by a few times, just to keep her company. Stell's like Jerry. Talks tough, but underneath she's really lonely. She likes me, says I make her laugh when she hasn't got much to laugh about. I feel good helping her. Is that wrong?"

"It's just that it doesn't look good for a police department employee to associate with a witness in a homicide investigation."

"We never talk about Jerry."

"Does she ask about our investigation?"

Now Wendy looks alarmed. "I don't know anything about the investigation. If I did, I wouldn't say a word, promise. I'm sorry, I should have asked permission. I don't want to make trouble."

"You're not making any trouble."

"Not a problem. I won't go back again."

"You don't have to do that," Pepper says. "The only thing I'd ask is maybe, if Stell says anything that would help with our investigation, you'd let me know. Me, not Tom."

Pepper stops in the hallway outside. "This is one of the things that makes me crazy about Tom. He has an opportunity right under his nose and he doesn't see it."

"Wendy's a person, not an opportunity. She's only willing to help you because she's terrified of losing her job."

"I know that. I'm just happy to have an inside connection. She's like a free CI."

"This is the second time you've taken advantage of her inability to say no. First you used her to persuade Stell to give you Shayla's address. Now you're asking her to spy for you."

"I'm not asking her to spy. I'm just asking her to keep doing what she was doing. And apparently enjoying. It's not like I'm telling her to break the law. All she has to do is play with the puppies and keep her ears open. For crap's sake, Doc, where's the harm in that?"

21

I snuggle down, put my feet on Frank's lap, angling for a foot rub. We're on the couch, in front of the fire, a blustery rain still hammering at the sides of the house. We're having what we call our "rosy scenario" talk, dreaming aloud about our future, making plans for our honeymoon.

"How about Paris?"

"Mmmm," Frank says. "I could take a cooking class."

"And I could gain a hundred pounds. What about the Caribbean?"

He shakes his head. "My ex and I went to Aruba on our honeymoon. Pick another place."

Frank and I don't talk much about our exes. I think about Mark more frequently now that I'm seeing Dr. Rogoff. Frank rarely talks about Shelly. They married young, myopically following the local tradition of marrying your high school sweetheart, getting pregnant and working on the family farm. Except Frank hated farming and Shelly wanted to be a nurse before she was a mother. Frank joined the Navy and was deployed to California. Shelly stayed home, went to nursing school. Frank loved the California weather and the laidback life style. Shelly loved being in Iowa. Long distance marriages don't work. Frank wasn't going to force Shelly to come to California and she wasn't going to force him to stay in Iowa. After three years being apart more than they were together, they divorced without kids or animosity. Last he heard, she'd married a doctor and moved to Hawaii.

My cell rings just as we're debating the merits of cruising to Alaska, Hawaii, or Mexico. Frank starts to tell me not to answer it and stops himself, knowing it will be futile. Raylene's voice slides through the phone, mellow and even. "We've had an incident."

Only Raylene made it through the pounding rain unscathed. Pence's gelled hair is hanging in limp strands. Pepper's spikey cut looks like a wilted palm tree. Two lieutenants, a sergeant, the shift commander, and a soaking wet Tom Rutgers are in the conference room huddled over cups of steaming coffee that Eddie Rimbauer is serving from his cart. My guess is that he has a scanner in his room, listening for any opportunity to show up at headquarters. Food and coffee being his ticket in the door.

"Thank Fran for the coffee, Eddie, and thank you for bringing it." Pence pours himself a cup.

"No problem, Chief. Glad to help out." Eddie doesn't move.

"You can leave now. We can help ourselves."

"I don't mind staying."

Eddie's deliberately misreading the cues or he's as obtuse sober as he was when he was drunk. Pence lowers his head like he's about to charge. It does the trick. Eddie scuttles out of the room promising to wait in the hallway to retrieve his cart. Pence motions for someone to shut the door.

"Tom, start us off."

Tom shakes his head. Drops of water roll down his temples. "Another fucking disaster. Pardon my French. We set up on the trailer about five o'clock. Watched for a couple of hours. There was a lot of traffic. Then right before we go in, a couple of johns try the door, can't get in and walk away. Then two of the girls leave the trailer, one of them still pulling on her pants. I wait another ten and knock on the door. The bitch in the baggy pajamas opens it. Starts yelling that she's going report me for harassment. I ask her about the johns and the two women. 'Oh,' she says,"—he raises his voice to a whiny sing song—"Them? They're from my book group.'" Tom scratches out a laugh. "I told you before, Chief. We got a leak."

Pence turns to Pepper. "What about your CI? She was going to warn you if there was a leak. What am I paying her for?"

"I've been trying to reach her cell, chief. No answer. Maybe she took the night off."

"What the. . . ?" Tom is shaking his head. "CIs don't get the night off!"

Pepper turns around. "You run your CIs your way, I'll do it mine. These women aren't slaves. They have lives."

"My guess is she's working both sides of the aisle. Collecting her salary from you and from Badger. She's probably the fricking leak."

"If she is, she has x-ray vision and fabulous hearing because she would have no way of knowing when you were going to do a raid. You didn't even tell me." Pepper hunches in her chair, arms folded across her chest, hands tucked underneath her arms.

Tom looks around the room. "No offense. But could we talk about this in a smaller group, Chief? Need to know only." Everyone but Pepper heads for the door.

"Dr. Meyerhoff," Tom stops me as I stand up. "I need you to stay."

I sit down. Tom is staring at me. "You think I'm the leak?"

"Not you. Mr. Coffee out there in the hall. The guy with

the big nose and big ears. Ever notice he's around here a lot? Anytime something goes wrong, there he is with his coffee cart, poking his nose into things. Think about it. He's a drunk."

"In recovery," I say.

"I know this guy. Worked with him for years. He's a major fuck up. Always has something up his sleeve. Not to mention that he's boning that little dispatcher."

"That's enough." Pence is on his feet. "We're tired and we all need to go back home and get some sleep." He turns to Tom. "When you have reliable evidence that Eddie Rimbauer or anyone else in my employ are complicit in thwarting these raids, bring it to me."

Pepper glares at Tom. "You should have told me about the raid. We're supposed to be working together."

"Dr. Meyerhoff," Pence snaps his briefcase closed and stands in front of me. "I'm aware that you and Mr. Rimbauer are close. If you learn anything, and I mean anything, that corroborates Officer Rutgers' suspicions, you are obligated to tell me." I open my mouth. He raises his hand. "I don't want to hear about confidentiality. I'm not in the mood. This is a dangerous situation involving the health and safety of my officers. Nothing more to say. Case closed."

Except that it isn't, not for me, not for Eddie. For all his troubles, I can't imagine Eddie doing anything that would put his fellow officers in jeopardy.

"Don't forget to eat something, ladies," Eddie says as Pepper and I walk into the hall. "Have to keep your strength up. Although you, my dear," he bows to Pepper, "could be starving to death and still knock me on my ass."

"Got that right. And I could do it with one hand."

She's smiling, but her eyes look tired. I wonder how often

she has to prove herself with the guys, how much it costs her to pretend that the constant commenting on her size is all in good fun. And what would happen to her if she stopped going along to get along?

"Here," Eddie says handing her a sandwich. "On the house." He hands me one and I wave him off. I'm going home to Frank who's probably just getting up and cooking breakfast. Eddie's going home alone to his room behind Fran's cafe. I haven't a clue who's waiting for Pepper when she goes home.

The rain has slowed to a drizzle and the sky is streaked with red from the rising sun. The streets are shiny and slick. My cell phone jangles. I don't answer. Traffic slows to a crawl, then stops entirely. Flashing lights from police and fire vehicles turn the pavement ahead into a lightshow of red, white and blue. I check my voice mail. I have two messages. One f,rom Frank who's leaving early for work and will see me later. The second is from Badger.

"Thanks for what you done. You didn't have to. All I really want is my son. Nothing else. Not to worry, I'll find a way to pay you back."

I grip the steering wheel, try to coordinate my breathing with the soothing swoosh and swipe of the windshield wipers. Pay me back for what? I haven't done anything. Is Badger so isolated, so starved for human contact, that he's turned a long ago tiny gesture of decency and our recent accidental prison contact into a grand romance? And if he has, what do I do about it?

22

Mother and I are in Nordstrom's. I tried to get out of shopping for a wedding dress by suggesting we go for a pedicure instead. Mother tells me all her friends love their mani-pedis, they're always asking her to go with them, but she can't. She keeps hearing my father's voice in her ears demanding to know how she dare patronize a place of mindless self-indulgence. A place where white women make women of color wash their feet.

This makes me wonder how she can justify my spending the equivalent of a year's worth of monthly mani-pedis on a tomato red silk sheath under an organdy duster with a stand-up collar. I love this dress. Even my mother likes it. I'm not so sure about my future Iowa in-laws who will expect to see me in something more traditional. Buying a red wedding dress is not to be taken lightly. I tell the saleswoman I need to think about it.

"What," says the saleswoman, smiling so hard there are cracks in her pancake makeup, "do we have in mind for the mother-of-the-bride?" I doubt the saleswoman has anything in mind beside a big sale and I resent her linguistically inserting herself into my wedding plans. She bends over my mother, poised to chuck her under the chin and tell her how cute she is. "Pearl gray to match your beautiful hair? Or something contrasting?"

My mother stands up. Not one to be played in the service of a sales commission, she backs up far enough to look the saleswoman in the eye. "I don't need a new dress."

The saleswoman droops. "This is your special day too. You should look as beautiful as your beautiful daughter."

"For your information, my special day has come and gone. I am not in competition with my daughter. Nor do I need to dress up like the queen of England to impress anyone." She turns to me. "What I do need is some lunch. Shopping among sycophants makes me ravenous."

The saleswoman looks confused, then brightens at the sight of another, younger shopper, who doesn't have her mother in tow.

We head for a French café overlooking a charming garden. I notice for the first time that we are no longer the same height. Both of us shorter than average all our lives and now, even in flat heels, I'm at least an inch taller than she is.

Mother puts her hand on my arm. "Let's go to the food court. It's cheaper. Plus, I don't need any phony French waiters hovering over me. Makes me nervous."

I'm about to spend big bucks on a wedding dress. Paying too much for lunch seems like nothing in comparison. But this is not the hill I want to die on. We've had a pleasant morning, not worth spoiling the good will between us arguing over a measly few dollars.

Food courts aren't what they used to be, a dreary collection of over-cooked steam table food. This one has soaring ceilings. An outside terrace filled with gigantic ceramic pots of flowering plants overlooking a fountain with a koi-filled pond. The seating is arranged to accommodate tables for group meetings and intimate parties of two. Cables bristle from the ubiquitous supply of UCB outlets. Servers, dressed in the costume of the country cuisine they represent, entice us with free tastes of food I barely recognize.

"There," my mother points to a small table next to a window. I tell her to hold the table, watch our purses, and I'll get the food. "Sit," she says, clutching her bag.

"I thought you were starving. What do you want to eat?"

"I've decided. I'm not going."

"To lunch?"

"To Iowa. To the wedding."

"Forget about the dress. Wear whatever makes you comfortable. The saleswoman was just angling for a sale."

"That's not why I'm not going."

"I thought you were happy Frank and I are getting married."

"I am. Very."

I have a slew of questions I want to ask her, but I know better. If I sit here quietly, give her some space, sooner or later, she'll open up. Bold as she can be with her opinions, asking for what she wants throws her into a panic.

"I won't feel comfortable in Iowa. And they won't feel comfortable with me. Better I should stay home."

"What do you mean you won't feel comfortable?"

She gives me a look. "Because I'm Jewish."

"So am I."

"That's different."

"Frank's family has been very welcoming to me. I've never felt any hostility from them. They don't care that I'm Jewish. They're more perplexed by the fact that I'm a psychologist and I don't eat ham."

"See," she says.

"See what? I also don't eat beef, veal, and lamb, only fish and chicken."

"Do they have any Jewish friends?"

She has a point. Before Frank brought me to Iowa, I doubt anyone in his family had ever knowingly talked to a Jewish person.

Mother leans across the table. "I wasn't going to tell you this But Sophie. You remember Sophie?"

Sophie, with her day-glow red hair and non-stop mouth, is my mother's closest friend and confidante. She probably knows more about my life than I do.

"She told me about a book she read about Jews in Iowa, how they started a big meat packing plant, very successful, until the people ran them out of town."

"The book was called *Postville*, Mother. And the Jews were Lubavitchers, an Orthodox sect so fanatical they would disown you and me in a minute. We're nothing like them and they were nowhere near where Frank's family lives."

"It starts somewhere. I remember how it was, you don't. And it's starting again, just like before." She leans forward and drops her voice. "You may think I'm being paranoid, but I'm not. This year alone, the Anti-Defamation League reports incidents of anti-Semitism increased by more than 50 percent. Don't tell me not to worry."

"I'm not telling you not to worry. I'm just saying you don't need to worry about Frank or his family."

I reach across the table for her hand, bony, brown-spotted and covered with ropey veins. For all her energy, her endless curiosity, my mother is getting old and it makes me sad.

"Is there something else bothering you, Mother?"

"I don't care if you're getting married in a church. It's okay if that's what Frank wants. I just don't think I'd be comfortable. No matter what kind of dress I was wearing."

She slumps slightly. I have no idea how long this has been bothering her.

"Frank hasn't been inside a church since he was married the first time. That was a long time ago. We haven't made any decisions about where in Iowa we're going to get married. Or who will marry us. Could be a judge or the county clerk. I'm surprised this matters to you. You haven't been inside a temple in years."

"That's because of your father. He hated religion. He was a cultural Jew, but not observant. Wouldn't even go to temple on High Holy Days. 'They just want my money,' he used to say, 'They don't give a damn about my soul.'"

"And you wanted to go?"

"Sometimes yes. Sometimes no. When I was a child my family went. Every Saturday."

"So why didn't you go by yourself if he didn't want to?"

"I did go sometimes, when your father was working. It wasn't worth it to make him mad. You know how he could be. This is something you're going to have to learn. Marriage is a lot of compromise."

"Couldn't you have found something that worked for the two of you?"

"Nothing about religion would have worked for your father. You know that."

"But why did he care what you did? Didn't he want you to be happy?" Something tightens along the ridge line above her eyes.

"I'm an old-fashioned woman. What made him happy, made me happy. Women today are different. Not better, just different. You expect some sort of parity in marriage. Women of my age knew better."

"What they knew was how to avoid conflict by having no needs of their own."

She pushes back from the table. "For God sakes, don't do that therapy thing with me. I'm your mother. I may be old. I don't have your education. And apparently, I didn't manage my marriage the way you think I should have. But you turned out alright, didn't you? Despite how your father and I messed things up." She's gripping her purse so tightly her knuckles are bloodless.

What's the matter with me? My mother is confiding in me, something she rarely does. Her fears are real to her, even if I think they are unrealistic. Do I listen? Am I compassionate? I'm fifty-two years old and I'm acting like a child because my Mommy won't come to my wedding. I need to remember to tell Doctor Rogoff. He'll be delighted.

"Doctor Meyerhoff?" A soft voice breaks our stony silence. "I hope I'm not interrupting."

I don't know if her timing is good or terrible, but the sight of Wendy pushing little Mysti in a stroller turns my mother's face from thunder clouds to cotton candy.

"What a cute baby. What's her name?"

"Mysti. M-Y-S-T-I."

Mother looks at me and rolls her eyes. It's an old complaint. Bad enough people give their children cute names, why do they have to muck up the spelling too?

"Such a cutie. I love babies. I was hoping for grandchildren of my own like my friends, but it's not to be." She looks sidelong at me, her cheeks flush with the pleasure of payback.

"It's Mysti's birthday soon. I have the day off. We were shopping for her present."

"Won't you sit down?" my mother says. "Maybe my daughter will remember her manners and introduce you."

Wendy looks at me, then at my mother. Clearly alert to

the sour vibe between us. "Mother, this is Wendy Scott. She works at KPD as a dispatcher. Wendy, this is my mother, Rivka Meyerhoff. She's visiting."

"Actually, we're shopping for a wedding dress," my mother says.

"Are you getting married?"

"Not me. My daughter."

"I thought you were married," Wendy says to me. "I mean since you're a counselor and I know you see couples."

This is a common misperception clients have about their therapists. Being well adjusted and happily married is not, never has been, a requirement for licensure. This makes me wonder about Dr. Rogoff. How, as he so boldly advertises on his website, he went from the pain of heartbreak to the joy of healing. Mysti gives a little cry of distress.

"She's hungry. It's way past her lunch time. I have apple juice and crackers in the stroller. We should go. She kinda makes a mess when she eats. I don't want to ruin your lunch." Wendy starts to get up.

"No, please don't get up." My mother puts her hand on Wendy's arm. "I want to buy lunch for everybody. A pre-birthday celebration for Mysti. It would be my pleasure." Wendy looks at me. I shrug. "They have everything here you could imagine. Maybe a little pudding or ice cream for the baby?"

Wendy asks for a tuna fish sandwich on white bread. My mother doesn't roll her eyes, although I'm sure she wants to. Tuna fish on white bread is not food in her culinary lexicon. Actually nothing served on white bread qualifies. I ask for Chinese chicken salad and my mother, ever the little professor, decides to model proper eating by declaring she has a yen for cottage cheese and peaches.

"Wendy and Mysti stay here. You," she says to me, "can help

me carry our lunches. In case you didn't notice, this is a food court, there is no waiter service."

Forty-five minutes later, my mother and Wendy are still bonding over baby stories. Neither one of them has eaten more than two bites of their lunch. Wendy is like an empath, highly sensitive to people in pain, especially older women who aren't her mother. I need to go to HQ. My mother wants to help Wendy with her shopping because there's nothing in the world cuter than little girl's clothes. Plus, she's going to steer Wendy away from Penny's and back to Nordstrom's where the clothes are better quality. And if Nordstrom's is pricier, she'll be happy to make up the difference. After all, it's not often she gets to buy presents for little girls. All her friends' grandchildren are already doctors and lawyers. Plus, when Frank and I are at work, she has nothing to do at our house but watch television and clean out the refrigerator because it hasn't been cleaned in a while. Not to worry, she says, she'll take a taxi home or maybe Wendy could drive her.

23

The minute I pull into the parking lot at headquarters I know something's wrong. Over in the corner, behind the mobile command center, I can see a knot of officers, Pepper's bunched red hair rising above the rest. I leave my coat and briefcase in the car and walk over. I can hear grunting, shuffling. I burrow in next to Pepper. Tom and Eddie are rolling around on the ground.

"It just started. Tom accused Eddie of being the leak and Eddie went after him. I tried to stop them, but Eddie pushed me off."

Tom flips Eddie on his back and straddles him. Eddie is breathing heavily, Tom barely at all.

"You crazy fucker. I'm half your age."

"I'm not the leak, you dick head." Eddie flails at Tom's head, managing only to whip up clouds of dust.

"Heads up. Here comes chaos," somebody whispers using the acronym for *chief has arrived on scene.*

Pence is running towards us as fast as he can without mussing his hair.

"What in hell is wrong with all of you. This is disgraceful. You're police officers, not thugs." He pulls Tom to his feet. His uniform is covered in dust and there's a trickle of blood on his ear. Eddie rolls to his knees and stays there, breathing heavily, drops of sweat exploding in the dust.

"Back to work, everybody." Pence is shouting. "Show's over. Nothing more to see here." He stabs at Tom's chest with his index finger. "In my office. Now."

"Right away Chief." Eddie struggles up on one knee.

"Not you," Pence's voice pitches high. "You're fired. Once and for all, done, finished, excommunicated." He pulls Tom by the arm, pushing him back toward the building.

Pepper and I move to help Eddie to his feet. He has a bloody lip and he's covered in dirt. He takes a step and winces. "Fucking knee." His cart is laying on its side in a puddle of coffee, crushing a large pink box of sopping wet pastries. Pepper tries to help him right the cart and he pushes her away. We watch in silence as he sets it back on its wheels, throws the box of pastries and ruined paper napkins into the trash and pushes off, limping badly.

24

By the time I get home, Frank and my mother are cooking dinner. She's showing him how to make kugel, a baked concoction of noodles, onion and cottage cheese. Tomorrow she promises to show him how to make apple strudel and chopped chicken liver. I go upstairs to change clothes and motion him to follow me.

"Is she driving you crazy?" I ask.

"Not yet. Maybe by the time she gets finished sharing old family recipes. It's a good thing I like to cook."

He leans over and gives me a kiss. "Good day? Bad day?"

"Some of each."

"Your mother had a great day."

"That's a surprise. She hated shopping. We had a big fight. I shot off my mouth, not for the first time, and hurt her feelings. Did she tell you she is not going to our wedding because Iowans are anti-Semitic?"

Frank sprawls on the bed watching me pull off my work clothes and pull on a pair of jeans and a sweatshirt. The way he looks at me, a combination of love, lust, and amusement makes me feel like Jell-O inside. Finding a man this handsome and sexy at my age is like winning the lottery without any of the disastrous consequences that follow an unexpected windfall.

"Who's Wendy?"

"She's a dispatcher. The woman who worked that fatal fire. We ran into her at lunch."

"According to your mother, Wendy and her daughter are not just the cutest, but Wendy is an amazing mother and she's doing it all by herself, no husband, no family."

"Wendy has a family. She lives with her mother and father."

Frank shrugs. "Just saying, your mother is so enamored with this woman I wouldn't be surprised if she started a GoFundMe campaign to send little Mysti to college."

At dinner, I wait for my mother to say something about Wendy. She has plenty to say about kugel, including a long dissertation on the role kugel plays in Jewish history, the difference between sweet and savory kugel, and the varieties of kugel to be found in Eastern Europe. Not a word about Wendy. It's a power play. She's holding out. Forcing me to ask. Frank tips his head, gives me a look and starts clearing the dishes.

"You ladies sit. Talk a little. I'm going to make coffee and rustle up some dessert."

Mother smashes her lips together.

"So, mother, how was your shopping trip with Wendy?"

"I thought you'd never ask." She pats her mouth with her napkin. Takes a sip of wine. "She's a lovely girl. Very brave. In my day, a single girl getting pregnant would never keep her child. I don't think it's right to have sex before marriage, but I'm a realist. Things happen. Men take advantage of women and then desert them after they get what they want. She's a good mother. Very loving. And little Mysti? An angel."

"Did you buy anything for them?"

"A few things. A toy and a dress. A nice sweater for Wendy who buys most of her clothes from the thrift store. How does a young girl like that learn to manage money so well?" She looks at me, waiting for my response. I hear the burble of the coffee pot, Frank loading the dishwasher, water running in the sink.

"She likes you very much, Dot. Told me about that terrible fire and how helpful you have been, giving her time off work, listening to her troubles." She reaches across the table and takes my hand. "I'm sorry I made that dig at you for not giving me grandchildren. I'm proud to hear how much you helped Wendy. My daughter, the doctor. Helping people. That's what gives life meaning. No doubt about it, you're your father's daughter."

25

The next morning, just like clockwork, Eddie is at the door to my HQ office with his coffee cart. Scrapes and bruises from the fight with Tom Rutgers mark his face.

"I thought you were fired."

"Me? No way. I'm the most important person in this whole damn department. Without me, there wouldn't be no coffee, no donuts." He wipes his hands on his apron. "I got a hold of my lawyer last night, negotiated a deal. He promises I can resign instead of being fired. Keep my pension. Sweet, huh? So now I work exclusively for Fran. And I got big plans. I'm going to expand the business with food trucks." He raises one arm, drawing letters on an invisible sign. "Picture this. Eddie's nuts, shriveled but sweet."

There is so much sadness in his face I can't bring myself to smile.

"Have a cup of coffee. On the house. It's the least I can do for being your most fucked up client."

"Maybe it's a new beginning, Eddie. You've been fighting to get back on the street for years. Odds of you winning that fight were pretty dismal from the start. At least now you can plan for the future."

He gives me a high five.

"My thoughts exactly, Doc. It's a blessing in disguise. Now, I have the two worst things a drunk can have. Time and money. Good thing they made me hand in my duty gun, so I won't be able to kill myself." Somebody passes in the hall. Gives Eddie a fist bump. "You watch, it'll take about a week and nobody will remember me." His phone buzzes with a text.

"Fran again. If she doesn't hear from me every five minutes, she thinks I pulled the plug out of the jug and I'm lying drunk in an alley. I gotta get back to the shop before she files a missing person's report." He turns his cart around. "Speaking of missing persons do you know where Wendy is? She didn't show up for work yesterday. And she don't return my calls."

"Funny I was going to ask you both the same question." I hear Raylene's voice before I see her walking toward my office.

"I saw her yesterday," I say. "She was with her daughter. Said she had the day off."

"According to a memo I just received from the personnel department, Wendy has applied for maternity leave. Did either of you know she was pregnant?"

Eddie's face turns as purple as his bruises. "Don't look at me. I had nothing to do with it."

I find Pepper in the report room, bent over a table. "Wendy was a no show for work yesterday. Raylene just told me she's applied for maternity leave."

"I'll be damned. Little Miss Sneaky Pants. Did you know she was pregnant?" I shake my head. "Wonder what else she's hiding. This is the twenty-first century. Unmarried mothers don't have to hide. Plus, she's already had one child out of wedlock."

"You don't know that she wasn't married to Mysti's father. All

I know is that, whoever he was, he's not involved in Wendy's life because that's the way she wants it."

Pepper pushes away from the table. Her cop face in full swing. "Why didn't she tell us earlier? What else hasn't she said? Liars don't stop at one lie."

"Number one, it wasn't any of our business." I stop, unable to think of reason number two.

"Nothing's off the table here. We're investigating a homicide.

Who knows, maybe Jerry is the father."

"That's preposterous. A man in a wheelchair, old enough to be her father?"

"Tom Rutgers says Eddie Rimbauer doesn't think age is a problem."

"Tom Rutgers?"

Pepper puts her hands up. "Just joking, Doc."

"I don't find any of this funny."

"Actually, neither do I." She fiddles with a fingernail. "Are you thinking what I'm thinking? That Wendy could be the leak?"

"No. Never occurred to me."

Pepper shrugs. "I got a funny feeling. Anything's possible." Before she says more, both our cell phones go off.

We line up like students in front of the principal. Pence is tapping his fingers on his desk, like we've kept him waiting. I can barely catch my breath after running up the stairs from the report room. Raylene and Tom are standing stiff as statues. Pence starts in on Raylene. How could she let this happen?

Doesn't she know what goes on in her dispatchers' private lives? Eddie Rimbauer is a worthless drunk, calculating, scheming. Why didn't she stop him from coming on to Wendy? Didn't she understand that as chief, he is liable for sexual harassment and creating a hostile work environment? Any minute now, Wendy could hire one of those "Excuse me for saying it" ball-busting female lawyers to sue him to Kingdom Come.

Raylene straightens the sleeves of her jacket. Years of responding to chaos and panic with a calm voice and a clear head have clothed her in Teflon for Pence's insults.

"Firstly, I have no idea who is the father of Wendy's unborn child. Secondly, as you well know, labor law forbids me from interfering in my employee's private lives. My employees are well aware of what constitutes harassment and that reporting it will not result in recriminations of any sort."

"Could Wendy be our leak?"

There's a crack in Raylene's composure. followed by a flash of anger.

"I have no reason to suspect Wendy of any wrongdoing. None at all. But, if she is the leak, as you allege, had you agreed to my many requests that you commission pre-employment psychological screening for dispatchers as well as officers, we might have had some advance warning of her anti-social tendencies, if she had any. Now, if you would like my resignation, you can have it."

Pence grabs her hand. "Raylene, for Pete's sake, I'm not asking you to resign. You are one of my most loyal employees. You've been here for as long as I've been here. My apologies. I was over the top. I'm under a lot of pressure. Everyone's on my case. Community groups, churches, the press, you name it. All of them screaming at me to solve this murder and get rid of the prostitutes."

"May I make a suggestion?" I raise my hand. Being treated like a child, I'm starting to behave like one.

"If I say no, will that stop you?" Pence lets go of Raylene's hand and walks to his desk.

"First thing," I say, "we have to find Wendy. Maybe she can

straighten things out. There could be a totally innocent explanation for her behavior. I'd like to be the one to look for her. We've spent a lot of time together since the fire. She trusts me. If you send Pepper or Tom to get her, she'll be too frightened to talk. She worries a lot about doing the wrong thing. The best approach is to reassure her that she's not in any trouble."

"Bad idea, Chief," Tom says. "Really bad idea. I've been on to Wendy since the beginning. She's our leak, no doubt. Send me."

Pence turns to Pepper. "I have to agree with Tom on this," she says. "I like the Doc, but truthfully, she's a little on the naïve side. Doesn't want to believe anything bad about anybody." She can't look at me as she says this.

Pence swivels toward Raylene for her opinion.

"I have to respectfully disagree with Tom and Pepper. I know Wendy and I know Dr. Meyerhoff. If you expect any cooperation from Wendy, you cannot treat her like a fugitive. Or a suspect. She's a scared young woman with an uncertain future. I think Dr. Meyerhoff is the right person for the job."

26

Early the next morning I'm in ticky-tacky territory, cheaply constructed houses, identical except for color. A snatch of song rushes at me. "Little Boxes" by Malvina Reynolds. I remember my mother singing it to me when I was a child. And then playing the record by folksinger Pete Seeger over and over.

Number 14 Bluebird Lane is mint green, with black shutters. A large clay pot sits on the front stoop planted with faded plastic flowers. The front lawn is Astroturf. Either the owners are seriously into conserving water in anticipation of another California drought or they hate gardening. I can hear voices inside, children's voices and music. A television. I use the knocker. Twice. The TV turns off and feet shuffle to the door. There's a slight movement at the peephole.

"Yes? Can I help you?"

"My name is Dr. Dot Meyerhoff from the Kenilworth Police Department."

A worn older version of Wendy opens the door wearing a flowered housecoat, short socks, and house slippers. No makeup, no jewelry. Pink scalp showing through her thinning blonde hair. Behind her and to the right, sitting on the floor surrounded by toys, is Mysti, transfixed by a soundless cartoon playing on an old color TV housed in a mahogany console.

"A doctor? Is something wrong? Is Wendy hurt?"

"No, nothing's wrong. I'm just making a routine house call. Is she here?"

Wendy's mother looks at Mysti, then back at me. She gestures me inside and shuts the door. The baby starts to whine. I hand her my business card. She studies it carefully.

"Wendy's at work. Told me she's been taking as much overtime as she can. Sleeping in the women's lounge at night."

"I'm afraid I didn't catch your name."

"Mildred. And this is Mysti, Wendy's daughter.

I follow her into the living room. Mysti whimpers. I'm a stranger. She's too young to remember we met once.

Mildred stoops, picks Mysti up with a small groan and settles in a tufted wing chair the color of mustard. "Have a seat." She points to a green velour sofa. "I'm too old for this. I don't know how I did it when Wendy was a baby." She looks at me like she's seeing me for the first time. "What kind of doctor makes house calls? No one make house calls anymore."

"I'm a psychologist. I counsel employees at the police department."

"Is Wendy in trouble?"

"No, no trouble. As I said, this is just a routine visit. A wellness check."

Mildred looks skeptical. "She's working too much I can tell you that. When she works overtime, so do I. And so does my husband. I told her to get a job working for a corporation that gives free childcare and free meals. She wouldn't listen. She had her heart set on working for the police. It was like there was no other job in the world."

Mysti starts to whine and squirm.

"Time for her nap. If she doesn't go down when she wants to there will be hell to pay all night." She sets Mysti on the floor. Hands her a stuffed lamb that bleats when she shakes it. "Cute, huh? It's Mysti's new favorite. She won't go to sleep without it. Wendy said she got it free the other day from some lady who likes babies." She stretches. Massages her lower back with her knuckles. "My back's killing me." She picks Mysti up, puts her on her lap.

"Sounds like Wendy is set in her ways."

"You don't know the half. I tried taking her to a counselor when she was in high school. She was skipping classes. Staying out late. She went twice to the counselor and refused to go back. When she got pregnant with Mysti, I wanted her to talk to someone. I told her she couldn't depend on me or her father for help. We're retired. Any money we have we need for ourselves. I tried to get her to think about an abortion or adoption. She didn't have to get married. But she wanted her baby to have a father." She jiggles Mysti and growls playfully in her ear. Mysti giggles, her rosy cheeks creased by two perfect dimples.

"I didn't know Wendy was married. Where is her husband?"

"Where he belongs. In prison. Bradenton Prison. For armed robbery. Wasn't even around when Mysti was born. Earns five cents an hour making mattresses. No child support. Nothing. The minute I met him, I knew he was no good. But Wendy does what Wendy wants.

"She told me not to tell anyone she was married. That's why you don't know. She was afraid she wouldn't get the job at the police station if anyone knew her husband was in prison. And she didn't want to get Weejay in trouble, like he didn't get into enough trouble on his own. I do everything for Mysti, but that no-good doesn't do a thing and Wendy still loves him. Worships the ground he walks on. Wouldn't take a breath without his permission." She shakes her head. "Willard. Willard Joy is his real name. But he wants everyone to call him Weejay, gets mad if you don't."

"Does Wendy visit him? Do they talk on the phone?"

"Wendy doesn't tell me what she does. I'm just her unpaid nanny. But I can tell you this, he says 'jump' and she does." Mildred shifts the baby to her other hip. "Little pipsqueak weighs a ton. I got to put her down for her nap. I'll tell Wendy you are looking for her." She starts for the door and turns around. "In case you're wondering, I love this baby more than anything, but somedays I wish Wendy had given her up to a stable family with a decent, hard-working father and a stay-at-home mother." She opens the door for me. "On the other hand, Wendy had a hard-working father and a stay-at-home mother. Look how she turned out."

"Some children are hard to raise," I say. She turns her head away, so I won't see her cry.

Pepper is sitting outside Mildred's house, her Harley parked at the curb, nose to nose with my car, the way cops meet up on the road so they can watch each other's backs without getting out of the driver's seat. She's high style in leather trousers, a fitted leather jacket, aviator glasses, and a stretchy red band around her hair.

"There's a law about wearing helmets," I say, "And about following people."

She grabs a bulbous full-face Darth Vader type helmet off the back of her bike. "I don't need this unless I'm moving. As you can see, I'm parked. And for your information, I'm not following you, I'm protecting you."

"From who? The only people in that house are a tired grandmother wearing bedroom slippers and a toddler."

"Just in case Wendy was home and did a runner. Can't quite picture you running after her in those."

She points to my flats, sensible, comfortable but not made for running. "Well, you wasted your time. Wendy, who, to my knowledge, is not yet officially a fugitive from the law, wasn't home. Her mother thought she was at work."

"Did you search the house?"

"Of course not. I'm not a cop and I don't have a warrant."

"That's why Pence should have sent me."

"I did learn something very interesting." I unlock my car door and stand next to it.

"Are you going to tell me what you found out or are you going to make me beg?" I don't say anything. "Sorry for what I said to Pence this morning. I should have kept my mouth shut. Mea culpa." She puts her palms together in a prayer position and bobs up and down. It's a weak apology, but I'll take what I can get. Truth is I can't wait to tell her.

"Wendy is married. Her husband's name is Willard Joy. Commonly known as Weejay. His current residence? Bradenton Prison. Same as Badger."

"You're kidding."

"Doesn't mean they know each other. There's almost four thousand prisoners in Bradenton."

"If there's an inmate with police connections, a guy like Badger is going to find him and have first dibs. Good work, Doctor. Your job performance exceeds expectations." She pretends to make a checkmark on an invisible clipboard. "I'm going back to HQ, make some phone calls, pull in a few chits, get a friend to check the visitors' log at Bradenton. First thing tomorrow we are going to look for the missing Miss Innocent."

"We?"

"You're the man. I'm not going anywhere without you."

27

I head home after work, the conversation with Wendy's mother doing hot laps in my head. Wendy's been lying to me and everyone else. Lied to get her job, lied about having time off, lied about not being married. I have a hundred unanswered questions. How far would she go? How far has she already gone? Her mother said Wendy would do whatever Weejay asked. More importantly, she didn't say what might happen to Wendy if she refused. Wendy's penchant for picking up strays like Jerry, Stell, even Eddie, combined with no boundaries, is a setup for disaster. Pepper and Tom think she's a fugitive and a crook. I'm wondering if she's a victim, fearful and slavishly obedient to her manipulative, abusive husband.

I pull into the garage, hungry, tired, and eager to see Frank's smiling face. My mother's gone home. We have the house to ourselves. The possibilities induce a quiver. Frank isn't cooking or smiling. He takes me by the arm and walks me into the kitchen. There's a huge bouquet of purple orchids sitting on the counter, still in the box.

"From your friend. The one who's locked up because he's too dangerous to live in civil society. There's a note attached. It's addressed to you. I don't open your mail without your permission." He pulls a stool out from the counter and watches me read, his chin resting on his hands.

The note is written in pencil on lined composition paper. One ragged edge roughly torn out of a notebook as though the writer was in a hurry. The printing is neat and small. There is no date.

Dear Doc,

I need your help. Before I die, I want my kid to know who I am and what I did for him. When I was 12, my old man went to the joint. I wrote to him. He never wrote back. I felt like a nobody. I don't want to do that to my kid. I'm asking you, forget that other stuff, find *my son, bring me a picture and an address."*

Badger

I hand the letter to Frank. He reads it. Grim-faced. "What other stuff?"

"I haven't a clue."

"You're not going to help him, are you? And you're going to tell Pepper and Pence about this?"

"Yes."

"When?"

"I don't know."

"What do you mean you don't know? You need to do it now."

"He's locked up. Almost two hours away. We're not in any danger."

"Why is he asking you? For crap sake, Dot. What's the matter with you? I'm scared. This guy sounds like he thinks you're a long-lost friend. Or the answer to his prayers."

"I keep remembering him from before. He was smart and

funny and sweet in his own way. He had a bad start in life. No mother, no father."

"Excuse me, I'm no psychologist, but I'll bet money that every orphan doesn't grow up to be a criminal. He chose his fate. He only gets so many years to blame his childhood, then when he screws up, it's on him."

"Being an orphan is different from being abandoned by two living parents. He was just a child. The only conclusion he could have come to was that he wasn't lovable enough for them to stay around. How big a loser do you have to be to be rejected by both your mother and your father? The fact that he understands how damaged he is and doesn't want to repeat it with his own son is a sign he's finally grown up. I understand why he was angry and self-destructive. He didn't have any support and he didn't know any better. Our brains only mature at twenty-five. Badger wasn't playing with a full deck."

"You're the one who's not playing with a full deck. I tolerate a lot from your work, but I will not, I repeat, will not, tolerate being put in danger. There's more wrong with this guy than low self-esteem. I'm only a dumb contractor but it's obvious to me, even if you can't see it, this guy isn't looking for a friend. You're being stalked."

28

"Wendy's at Stell's. I know it in my gut." Pepper's working out on a rowing machine in the headquarters gym, sweat dripping off her chin and down her neck. The muscles of her back and shoulders, visible under her tank top, still bear definition from her days as a competitive swimmer. I'm reclining motionless on the seat of a recumbent bicycle, drinking a latte and eating a bagel. It's seven-thirty in the morning. Pepper's been exercising for nearly an hour. She keeps urging me to work out, get in shape, promising the rewards in energy are worth the effort. She offers to design a program for me. I wonder if she's been talking to my mother who thinks I'd make a more beautiful bride if I lost five pounds and tightened up a little. She too offers to share her very own custom-made exercise plan, developed specifically for her by the fitness trainer at her senior living facility. So far as she's ever said, his only known qualification is that he is really a "hunk."

"She's not at her mother's, you've already been there. Her old man's in jail. Where else would she be?" Pepper stands, mops at her face and hair with a towel. "Give me a minute to jump in the shower. Then let's hop over to Mateo Park and pay Miss Stell a visit. I'll bet you ten bucks we find Wendy." She stops on her way to the locker room. “You alright? You don’t look so good; you’re a little green around the gills.”

That’s an apt description. I hardly slept at all last night. I hate fighting with Frank. He’s right. I know he’s right. I will have to tell Pepper about Badger’s letters. Just not today. I can’t explain my reticence. Clinical intuition maybe, but something makes me want to hold off, see what happens. Maybe this goes away. Maybe it doesn’t. Maybe Pepper can use Badger’s search for his son as leverage to get him to confess to Jerry’s murder. But not today. Not when she’s this amped up and Wendy is still missing and possibly in danger.

The Sammies start barking the minute we approach Stell’s mobile home. Pepper knocks on the door. Hard. No response. She does it again. The harder she knocks, the louder the Sammies bark, back and forth like a chorus of call and response. I’m shivering. Pepper, still flush from her workout, is bundled in a down vest, her damp hair sticking out in all directions. There’s a cold wind blowing, rattling the dead leaves that litter the ground. I look around. The narrow lanes between mobile homes are mostly clear of refuse, the recycling bins neatly placed inside their wooden racks.

“Now what?” Stell cracks the door open. She’s barefoot, dressed in a tan velour jogging suit. She must have a closet full in every conceivable color.

“Good morning, Stell,” Pepper is smiling. “Sorry to barge in, but we need a minute of your time. Won’t take long.”

“Unless you’re from Publishers Clearing House and I’m the first prize winner, I haven’t got any time.”

“We’re looking for Wendy. Being that you’re BFFs, we thought she might be here. We’re concerned because she hasn’t shown up for work.”

"Sorry. I have no idea where she is."

"Not that I think you'd lie, but it would be best if I could come in and look around, just to be sure she isn't hiding somewhere without your knowledge."

"Like where would that be? I live in a mobile home, not the Taj Mahal."

"Let them in. It's okay." Wendy's voice floats from inside.

Pepper winks at me and mouths the words "You owe me ten."

Stell shuts the door. I can hear her and Wendy talking. Their voices barely audible over the wind. The door opens. The look on Stell's face is not hospitable. "I think this is a lousy idea, but it's her decision."

To be blunt, Wendy looks like shit. Even Pepper startles at her hollow, once plump, cheeks. The deep blotchy depressions under her eyes. The dogs circle my feet, sniffing. I silently dare one to lift a leg.

"Sorry, no place to sit," Stell says as she plops into a plastic lawn chair and folds her arms over her chest. Wendy is lying on a sagging sofa that has been made into a bed. She's wearing an oversized black t-shirt and flannel sleep pants decorated with Christmas trees.

"You don't look well," I say. "Raylene told us you're pregnant. Do you need medical attention?"

Wendy looks at Stell who raises her hands in surrender. "Up to you. It's your life."

"I had an abortion. Stell's taking care of me. She was a nurse."

"Care to tell us who the father is? Or who performed the abortion?"

"Hold up, Pepper," I say. "Before you start asking questions, let's give Wendy a minute to adjust to the fact that we just barged in here with no warning."

Pepper glares at me. Stell glares at Pepper.

"I'm not here to judge," Pepper says, "I don't care who the father is, I just need his name. For information purposes."

"Not here to judge? Bullshit. You cops think you're judge and jury." Stell is on her feet sending the dogs into a state of high dudgeon. "That other cop, arrogant dude with a mustache, threatened me with jail. Had the nerve to tell me it's my fault Jerry's dead because I didn't keep this place clean. I told him my job is to collect rents, not pick up garbage. The slobs who live here have to pick up after themselves, I'm not their fucking mother." Stell starts to paw through her pockets. The minute she does Pepper rests her hand on her gun. "I told that other cop I was housebound the whole week before the fire. All the Sammies had viral enteritis. Crapping all over the place. I couldn't go out."

"I thought you took Jerry's dog to the vet the day before the fire," I say.

"I thought you said you were a psychologist."

"I am."

"You sound more like a cop." She turns back to Pepper. "I told mustache man before the fire, I saw gang bangers driving around here with their tinted windows. Making noise like they was throwing things around." She pulls a wrinkled pack of cigarettes out of her pocket, walks to the door, opens it, and lights up, blowing a gust of smoke out toward the road.

Pepper lets go of her weapon. Stretches her cramped fingers. "Why didn't you call us when you saw the gang bangers?"

"For what? They'd be gone before you people finished your donuts and coffee."

Pepper rolls her eyes and turns to Wendy. Her voice softening. "Let's start again. Wendy, you do know you're in trouble, don't you?"

"Because I had an abortion?"

"Because you failed to show up for your shift without calling in." I wait for Pepper to roll out the list of Wendy's other wrong doings, like being married to a felon and lying about it. She sits next to Wendy on the couch. It squeaks and seesaws under her weight. "Help me out and I'll put in a good word for you."

"Help you out how?"

Stell shouts over her shoulder. "Don't tell them anything. Get a lawyer."

"Let's start with what Stell doesn't want you to tell us."

Wendy's voice pitches into a watery soprano. "I don't know what Stell's talking about. Really, I don't. I haven't done anything wrong. Getting pregnant is not against the law."

Stell bangs back into the room. "She's sick. Can't you leave her alone? She could have an infection. She's lost blood. Look at her, does she look right to you?"

Wendy shifts her position and winces. "Stell's a nurse," she announces this for the second time.

"Good," Pepper says. "Because I'm pretty sure it's legal for nurses to perform abortions."

"I didn't say Stell did the abortion." Wendy looks panicked.

Pepper pulls her smart phone out of her vest pocket. "I'll just take a minute to validate that Stell's license is up-to-date."

Stell throws her lit cigarette out the door, walks to a small desk in the corner and shuffles through a stack of papers. "Here. Save yourself some trouble." She shoves a piece of paper at Pepper.

Pepper squints as she reads. "What a surprise. You *are* an up-to-date licensed vocational nurse. An LVN. Congratulations. I believe that qualifies you to empty bedpans and wash people's butts."

Pepper starts typing on her cell phone with the nimble thumbs of someone who has grown up with a pacifier in her mouth and a smartphone in both hands. She smiles and begins to read aloud. "*The performance of an abortion is unauthorized if the following is true: (a) The person performing the abortion is not an authorized health care provider pursuant to Section 2253 of the Business and Professions Code. Authorized is defined as a registered nurse or a doctor.*" Do you have another license as an RN? If you do, I'd like to see it, please. Take your time. I sure hope the Sammies didn't eat it."

Stell marches down a short narrow hallway that leads to the back of the trailer. I hear a door slam. The Sammies rush after her, yelping and scratching their nails on the floor.

"I don't want to get Stell in any trouble. She's my friend. She helped me. I was scared. I didn't have any money to go to a hospital. I was thinking of killing myself. You don't know what it's like being me."

"You got that right," Pepper says, half-under her breath, half to me. "Back to my original question. Tell us who the father is. It will go better for you if you tell us voluntarily."

"What difference does it make to you who the father is? Was."

"Because I'd like to believe that we're on the same team, the KPD team." Pepper winks at me over Wendy's shoulder."

Wendy pushes back against the sofa. Her face blank except for a snail trail of tears under each eye.

"I'm disappointed," Pepper says. "I just offered you an opportunity to make things better for yourself and you're not interested. That leaves me no choice but to lay my cards on the table. I had a surprise the other day and I don't like surprises. I looked over a list of names of people who recently visited Bradenton Prison. What a surprise to find your name on the list. Wendy Scott. Do you have any idea why your name would be on the list? Who you might be visiting?"

Wendy shrugs. "It's a common name. There's lots of Wendy Scotts."

Pepper slaps her hands on her thighs. "That's it. It's your evil twin. Now why didn't I think of that?"

I don't like this side of Pepper. She's enjoying herself, like a cat tormenting a half-dead mouse.

"This Wendy Scott—by the way, her driver's license photo looks remarkably like you—was there to have a conjugal visit. Conjugal visits are only permitted for married inmates. Let's see . . ." Pepper counts on her fingers. "Now if that visit resulted in a pregnancy then that Wendy Scott should be about six weeks pregnant. Her husband, with the ironic name of Willard Joy, aka Weejay, spreads happiness throughout the world selling drugs and redistributing wealth by means of armed residential burglary."

"Stop it." Stell slams out of the back. The Sammies crowding behind her. "Get out. This is my house. You need a warrant."

"I don't need a warrant to interview an employee of KPD."

"You need a warrant to do it in my house."

"Wait a minute, please, wait a minute." I'm on my feet. "Let's slow things down, can we?" I look at Pepper.

"Okay with me, Doc. I got all the time in the world." Pepper does not look happy that I'm interfering but at least she doesn't tell me to shut up and sit down.

"I'm sure Pepper doesn't mean to come on this strong. She's desperate to solve a serious crime and just wants to get to the bottom of things before anyone else gets hurt. When someone is so totally focused on getting results, they can forget that people have feelings and don't like to be ordered around. Or threatened."

"You think?" Stell is leaning against the door, her hand on the knob.

Pepper stands. "The doc's right. My apologies. It's a bad habit of mine. Like the doc says, sometimes I get too involved, only because I'm afraid for you, Wendy. I think you may be mixed up in something or with someone who could get you hurt. I don't want that to happen. Same for you, Stell, I don't want you to get hurt either."

"You don't give a rat's you-know-what about me. You threatened me with jail."

"I should never have said that. I have no intention of arresting you. You may have done something illegal, I won't lie, but I know that what you did you did out of compassion for Wendy. And you probably did it as well as any hospital. I can tell people that. So can Wendy.

"But, here's the thing. Wendy's in deep trouble. I don't know with who or even how deep. She's married to a convicted felon and lied about it on her employment application. That's against the law."

"But I didn't lie." Wendy is twisting the bottom of her t-shirt into a knot. "When the background investigators asked if I knew any felons, I said I knew somebody I met in high school. They didn't ask if I married him, so I didn't say."

"Associating with a known felon when you work in a police department, and not telling anyone about it, is a serious offense."

"See. That's why I had to have an abortion. I didn't want people asking who the father was."

"Your husband is in the same prison with the man we think is responsible for Jerry's death."

"There are a lot of people in that prison."

"Exactly. I need to make certain that your husband and that man don't know each other, so I can eliminate him from our inquiries. All you need to do to help him is answer a few questions for me. That's all. Easy-peasy."

"Weejay would never hurt anyone. He has an addiction. He's

working on it in a prison drug program. I don't want to get him kicked out of the program."

"Of course, you don't. Especially now that he's trying to clean up." Pepper gives an exaggerated sigh. "I apologize for pushing you. I don't meet people like you very often, someone so loyal she is willing to put her husband's welfare in front of her own interests."

"Let's take a break. I need to talk to the chief. He's been on my back. Everybody wants to know who murdered Jerry. But now that we know where you are, that you're safe, we can take a breather." Pepper sighs again. Wipes her hands on her jeans. Beads of sweat dot her forehead. She's been backpedaling so fast it qualifies as aerobic exercise. "How about we meet tomorrow morning, bright and early. We'll all be calmer and rested. Me included. Okay with you, Wendy?"

"Can Stell come?"

"Of course," Pepper says. "Bring anyone you want. Even the Sammies."

Pepper starts the car without putting on her seat belt and drives off sending a pile of dead leaves into the air.

"That was a real about face you did. I'm glad you did it. I didn't like the way you were treating Wendy. You were unnecessarily cruel."

"I wasn't being cruel. I was being strategic. Everyone expects the good cop/bad cop routine. But when one cop plays both sides, it throws them off. They don't know what to expect and when that happens, you move in for the kill. Or perhaps you would prefer another word like resolution or closure." We come to a stop sign. Pepper clicks her seat belt closed. "Wendy's a professional victim. At the same time, she's a user. She's playing us and playing Stell."

"Aren't you afraid she's not going to show up tomorrow?"

"Wendy's not going anywhere without Stell's help. Plus, she'll get her kid first. As for Nurse Rachet, she'd do anything to avoid jail time, including throwing Wendy under the bus, because if she goes to jail who takes care of the Sammies? She cooks for them, for God sake. Did you see one can of commercial dog food anywhere? Come to the interview. You'll see how fast they'll turn on each other to save their own necks."

29

The morning sun is high. The commute traffic has thinned to a trickle. I'm in my car, halfway between home and my private office when my cell phone starts buzzing like a trapped insect. I pull to the side of the road because I haven't yet mastered this hands-free Bluetooth thing. I have two messages from Fran, frantic with worry because she can't find Eddie. His bed hasn't been slept in and he didn't show up to work this morning. She's absolutely convinced he's on a bender and if we don't find him soon, he'll kill himself.

The other message is from Pepper. Her voice is strained. Wendy was a no-show for her early morning appointment. She's not at her mother's and she's not at Stell's. Pepper knows this because, despite Stell's threatening her with a lawsuit for brutality, she searched every inch of the mobile home and found nothing but dog hair. If Wendy or Eddie contact me, I should call 911 and be very careful, because, as of thirty minutes ago, Wendy and Eddie may be persons-of-interest in, not one, but two murders. She starts to explain. We lose connection. I ditch my pre-employment reports and head straight for headquarters.

***

Raylene is standing in the hall, staring at the door to my office. There's something off about her usual runway ready appearance.

"A patrol unit found a body by the creek that runs behind the Mateo Trailer Court. A woman's body. Very young. Badly beaten. Tom and Pepper are working the scene. Given the victim's tattoos, it's probably Pepper's confidential informant." She pauses. Takes a deep breath. "You know that Wendy failed to keep her appointment with Pepper this morning. She's not answering my calls. I hope to God she's not involved in this young woman's death. If you hear from her. Let me know ASAP. I'll do the same." She walks away.

I put my briefcase down as my cell phone goes off. Eddie's name is on the screen.

"Eddie. Where are you? Fran is frantic."

"Not to worry. I'm good."

"Are you with Wendy?"

"No comment. Taking the fifth instead of drinking it."

"That's not funny. People are looking for both of you. They just found a dead body by the creek."

"That's why I'm calling and why I'm going to hang up as soon as I finish saying what I want to say. Page one of the textbook on handling confidential informants is never sleep with your CI."

"What are you talking about?"

"The dead hooker is Tom Rutgers's punch. That's what you get when you put an egg sucking dog in the hen house." He hangs up.

"Let the crime scene folks do their job." Pence, perched on the edge of his desk is, as usual, at his sartorial best. Pepper, still wearing her blue police windbreaker over her jeans and sweatshirt, looks stunned. Tom looks somber. "I've asked the doctor to join us because." He pauses for a minute, trying to remember why he wanted me here. I angle my chair to better see Tom's and Pepper's faces.

"I don't need a psychologist." Pepper doesn't look at me. "I need to nail the piece of crap who did this. She was a kid. A fucking kid." She hits her hands on the arms of her chair. "Let's go. I want to talk to Badger." She starts to get up. Tom follows.

"Sit down. Both of you. That's an order." Pence is on his feet in full cop mode. His voice raised, his stance bladed, and his finger pointed. "This is the second homicide in two months. The press has questions, so does the community and I'm the one who has to have the answers. I need information." He turns avuncular again. "I know you want to get to the bottom of this. And you will. I have faith. In both of you." He leans against the edge of his desk. Composed, almost casual. "This is not your fault, Pepper. Let me remind you that your confidential informant lived a dangerous life. She is not an innocent victim."

"I know who's behind this. We all do. Badger."

"Be that as it may," Pence says, "I cannot accuse an incarcerated inmate of murder. He is locked up miles from the scene. I'd sound like I lost my marbles."

"Not Badger in person. One of his so-called devoted followers."

"Even still, we have no evidence connecting anyone to this crime. This is America. People are innocent until proven guilty. In five minutes, I need to be out in front of the press. Five minutes. I need you to give me something to say."

I lean over and tap Pepper on the shoulder. "Tell the chief about your CI. Make her more human to the press, less of a statistic. Maybe start with her real name."

"Everyone called her Pixie because she was so small. Her real name is Ronda."

"How many times have you used her as your CI?" Pence is taking notes.

"Two. Maybe three. The first time was after I picked her up for shoplifting. Third offense. She was facing jail time."

I draw my chair a little closer. "Say something about her background. You told me about it, but the chief doesn't know."

"Typical story. Father screwing her for years. She tells her mother. Mother doesn't believe her. Slaps her around. She runs away. Lives on the street. Smokes a little dope. Starts hooking. Stripping."

Pence scribbles something on his notepad. "So, she's a hooker and a hype?"

Pepper's face blazes. "She's a human fucking being. She smokes a little weed, so what? It's not like heroin. What century are you living in?" She pushes back in her chair. The scraping sound sends shivers up my spine. "Until this morning, nobody knew I had a CI working the massage gig. Nobody but you three." Pepper points at the chief, at Tom, and at me. "Want to tell me which one of you leaked it to Badger?"

Eddie knew about the CI. Not more than an hour ago he told me Pixie was Tom's girlfriend.

Tom's face is redder than Pepper's. "I'd never give up a CI. Never. Let's go. It's a long drive to Bradenton."

Pepper turns to Pence, facing him full on. "Want to know what to tell the press, Chief?" He nods, his pen poised over his notepad. "Tell them Pixie would still be alive if I had arrested her on the shoplifting beef and thrown her in jail. The way I feel, I might as well have killed her myself."

30

"Well?"

"Well what?"

"What looks good to you?"

"Everything. What looks good to you?"

Frank shrugs. We're trying a new Latin restaurant with cuisine from Salvador, Peru, Chile, Brazil, Ecuador, Mexico, and Guatemala. Since our fight over Badger, we've barely talked. I thought eating out would be better than eating at home. In a restaurant if we can't talk to each other, we can at least talk to the waiter.

"How was your day?" I ask. "Anything new to report?" A tepid attempt at conversation, but it's the best I've got.

"Your mother called. She wants to know if you made up your mind about the red wedding dress and to complain she isn't sleeping well because she's getting a lot of middle-of-the-night robo calls. I told her I'd get her a call blocker."

"What's a call blocker?"

"A gadget you plug into your phone. Stops unwanted calls."

"That's nice. Thanks. She'll appreciate it."

We dive back into our menus. A waiter with shining boot black hair and a practiced smile asks for our order.

"Let's start with pisco sours and a ceviche sampler. Okay with you, Dot?"

I nod. It's the first thing we've agreed on in days.

"And how was your day?" he asks. "Anything new with you?"

Without warning, I start to tear up. The waiter arrives with our food and drinks. One look at my face and he asks if there is something wrong with his service. Or the food. Frank shoos him off and reaches across the table for my hand.

"Talk to me Dot. What's going on?"

"Eddie's disappeared. Along with Wendy, the dispatcher."

"Good for him, the rascal. He's always struck me as a lonely guy who needs a woman."

"They're persons-of-interest in two murders. The man who burned to death in his trailer. And, as of this morning, a young woman who was working for Pepper as a confidential informant."

"Does any of this have something to do with that Badger guy?"

"Pepper thinks so."

The waiter puts a basket of plantain chips on the table. "On the house," he says and whisks away.

"I've been trying to help Wendy. Ever since she took the trailer fire call. Now I find out she's been lying and not just to me. Same for Eddie. He's lying too and I don't know why. It scares me."

Frank runs his thumb over my cheeks. "Your mascara's running into the ceviche."

"Pepper, poor Pepper, thinks it's her fault that young girl was murdered. If you could have seen the look on her face. She's going through hell."

"Does she really think Eddie or Wendy is capable of murder? Do you?"

"Under the right circumstances," I say, "anyone's capable of murder."

31

The next morning Pepper knocks on the door to my HQ office while I'm finishing up two of the pre-employment screening reports I didn't finish yesterday. She doesn't look well.

"I feel like crap. I'm going home."

"Good idea. You look terrible."

"Close quarters in the interview room with Tom and Badger and I'm the one who gets sick. Tom is on the job and Badger's probably out in the yard pumping iron. Healthy as a horse."

She may be sick, but my guess is that she's also suffering with survivor's guilt. Stress compromises the immune system. Pepper's a woman in a man's world. Any display of emotion equals weakness. Better to catch a cold than to admit your red eyes and red nose come from crying over your dead informant. She flops into a chair, grabs a handful of tissues from the box on my desk and blows her nose.

"Badger stonewalled us. Doesn't know nothing about nothing. I showed him a picture of Pixie's body. Know what the bastard said? 'I prefer women who move.' I came unglued. If I hadn't checked my weapon, I think I would have shot him. He's lucky I didn't try with my bare hands." She puts her palm on her forehead and pronounces herself burning up. "I don't care if he was in solitary with no phone and his mouth taped shut, Badger is behind Pixie's murder. Question is, how did he know about her?" Her face is white. Clammy. Beads of sweat mark her forehead.

"You need to go home. You're sick. I'm worried about you."

"If you're so freaking worried about me, why didn't you tell me you and Badger were now buddies."

"What are you talking about?"

"We were getting ready to shut the interview down when Badger asked about you. Wanted to know why you didn't come with me and Tom. I told him you were never coming back to see him. He told me I was wrong. That you'd be back because you and he had a special bond going back years."

"You already know about that. You were there when we talked about it. We met at the homeless shelter. He was a kid. I was a grad student."

"He said you were helping him, doing phone therapy. What's he talking about?"

"I told you, he sent me flowers. And a note asking me to help him find his son."

She grabs the cell phone off the top of my desk before I can stop her. Does something with her fingers. "There are two calls on here from him. Phone therapy? When were you going to tell me about them? Or weren't you?"

"Stop treating me like a suspect."

"Stop acting like one."

"He's called me twice, left messages. Same as always. He wants me to help him find his son. I didn't call him back, I didn't talk to him. I figured he'd stop if I don't respond."

She pushes my phone at me. "When he calls again—because he will—I set your phone up to record any conversations." She points to a red square with a tiny white phone in the middle.

"Tap this. Then call me." She zippers her jacket. "You are so naïve, Doc. When a guy like Badger wants something, he won't stop until he gets it. You could say no a thousand times, he'll find some way to make you do it."

"Like what? Report me to the Psychology Board?"

"You have no idea how long this creep's tentacles are. I'll bet you big bucks he has Wendy's husband on his payroll. He denied it, of course. And I quote: 'That little prick? Never met him.'" She walks to the door.

"Did you talk to Weejay?"

"Turns out he was transferred to The California Conservation Center at Susanville. For his own safety. I called Susanville to arrange a visit. The place is on lockdown after three inmates did a walk-away. One of them being the recently arrived Willard Weejay Joy."

The unctous female voice trapped inside my cell phone pleasantly informs me that I have three new messages and no saved ones. The first is from Fran, telling me what I already know, that Eddie is still missing. She is frantic with worry. The second is from Frank reminding me he has a photography class this evening. The third is from Badger wanting me to know that his prison pit-bull act isn't the real him. It's how he stays alive. I shouldn't be influenced by whatever the red-headed Amazon says about him after yesterday's interview. The way he is with me is the real him.

32

As soon as I finish the last pre-employment report, I head to Dr. Rogoff's office for my third appointment. The door is open. I can see him pacing, looking at his watch. I'm twenty minutes late and totally not ready to listen to him interpret the meaning of my tardiness. I peek around the door.

"Sorry I'm late. Police business."

He sits. "Whether you're late or not is your business, not mine. I still charge for the entire hour."

He stares at me. I stare back. I haven't been thinking about therapy at all. Too much Wendy in my life, too much Pepper, too much Eddie and too much Badger. Therapy works best when the client spends time between sessions contemplating the issues raised by her therapist. Or keeps a journal. Or records her dreams.

"Nothing to say? Perhaps you'd like me to ask you a question."

"That would be helpful. My mind's blank."

"Well then, how about talking over what brought you here in the first place? How are things going with your fiancé?"

I tell him about my fight with Frank. Tell him I think I have compassion fatigue. That I'm so concerned about the people I work with, I have very little empathy for Frank's feelings.

"Compassion fatigue? That's how you rationalize pushing Frank away?"

"Let me guess? You think I push him away because my ex left me for another woman." I sound whiny, even to myself.

"Being abandoned is reason enough to not trust or to be more discriminating in the future. But pushing someone away is different. It's a hostile action."

"I'm not hostile. I get irritated with him from time to time, but I'm never hostile." There's a burning sensation in my chest that suggests this may not be accurate.

"I suppose you're also not feeling defensive at the moment."

The burning sensation intensifies. First a campfire, now the entire forest is in flames.

"If you're not mad at me or at Frank, then who are you mad at?"

"You want me to say I'm mad at my father."

"Are you?"

"He's dead."

Dr. Rogoff closes his eyes, temples his hands and starts tapping his fingertips together. A minute passes. He opens his eyes and looks at his watch. The room is so quiet I can hear the clock ticking and the furnace turning on and off. He angles his chair away from me, surreptitiously trying to read a letter laying open on his desk. He's either purposively trying to aggravate me or he's totally checked out, biding his time until I pay him. The longer he sits in silence, the madder I get. The madder I get, the more juvenile I feel.

"Alright," I say. "I give up. What is this, a therapeutic stand-off? I am not paying you to ignore me."

"Ah, so now you are mad at me."

"Why wouldn't I be? You're being provocative. This is childish." To be childish is a condemnation. To be childlike is to repeat a behavior learned first in childhood. I'm not sure which one fits me best.

"Like your father provoked you?"

"You're nothing like my father. My father was a champion of the underdog. He would never ignore someone in pain."

"Pain? Are you in pain? You don't look like you're in pain. You don't sound like you're in pain. I hear what you think about pain, but I can't tell when you feel it."

I start to defend myself and choke on a huge, gulping, gut wrenching sob. Rogoff waits. Doesn't offer me tissues. He just sits. I get up and help myself to a great wad of tissues from a mother-of-pearl holder sitting on a bookcase.

"Where's this from?" I ask. He looks at me over the top of his glasses. "No small talk allowed?"

"No deflection," he says, using the therapy term for changing the subject to avoid a painful topic.

Out it comes. I tell him I worry that I am like my father. Boundless empathy for those in distress while cheating the people closest to me of my time and attention. He nods his head, but slightly, not wanting to convey agreement that would prompt me to seek his continued approval. He rests his chin in the curve between his thumb and index finger, as though thinking deeply. Presses his lips together to keep from talking. Silence is a therapist's ally. An empty pause that creates so much discomfort the client is literally forced to continue speaking, no matter how painful the disclosure.

"My father's preoccupation with great causes was the source of constant problems. He thought nothing of lecturing my mother and me for hours on end. His so-called anti-corporate principles mired us in poverty. All the while he tyrannized us with his perpetual identity as a victim." Rogoff keeps nodding his head, as though listening to music only he can hear. I walk across the room and sink to my seat hugging the entire box of tissues to my chest. “Well that was cathartic,” I say.

Rogoff smiles. “Indeed,” he says. “Tell me more.”

33

I drive home slowly as dusk settles on the road. My swollen eyes splinter the oncoming headlights into blurry fragments. I hope Frank won't notice or ask questions. I check my face in the rear-view mirror before going inside. If I move fast, I'll have time to repair my make-up before he gets home from his photography class. A car pulls up behind me and noses so far into the garage that I can't lower the door. The glare of the headlights makes it impossible to see who's driving.

"Frank?" I yell at the darkness. A bulky man rushes me, pushes me out of the way. Another smaller figure runs past and crouches in front of the still gurgling grill of my car.

"Is that you, Eddie?" I turn around. "Who's with you?"

The motion detector lights in the driveway flash on and off as Frank pulls up in his truck, blocking Eddie's car. He jumps from the driver's seat. "What's going on?"

Eddie runs towards him. "Move your truck."

"Not until you tell me what's going on."

There's a whimper behind me. I flick on the garage lights. Wendy is flattening herself against a packing crate full of books.

Eddie rushes back into the garage. He's panting hard and his face is red and sweaty.

"It's fucking Badger. I need to move my car. I'll be back in a minute. Take Wendy inside. You okay, kid?" Her only answer is a snuffle.

"Badger's in prison. He can't be following you," I say.

"Not him personally, his flunky gang bangers."

Frank grabs Eddie by the shirt. "You're being followed by a gang of thugs and you led them to my house?"

Eddie rips away. "I lost them. I know how to fucking shake a tail. That's why I need to hide the car before they figure out where they lost me. Move your damn truck."

"How do you know your car doesn't have one of those tracking devices?"

"What do you think, contractor man, I'm as stupid as them? It's a rental. I just got it." He steps toward Frank. "Now move."

"I'll do better than that," Frank says. "I'll follow you. Make sure you hide the car. Then I'll drive you back here so I can beat the crap out of you for putting Dot and me in danger."

I wrap Wendy up in blanket and park her on the couch with a cup of hot tea and a box of tissues. I don't know if it's fear or cold, but she's shaking like a leaf. I turn up the heat. There's a squeaking sound as the garage door rolls up, then down. Wendy and I both jump. Frank and Eddie walk into the room, Eddie first, Frank behind him. His face curled in anger. He shoves Eddie into a chair.

"Don't move. Don't speak."

"Whoa, contractor man. You'd a made a good cop, know that?" Frank raises his arm, bent at the elbow, ready to strike. Eddie lifts both his hands in mock surrender.

"You think this is funny?" Frank looks at me. His eyes are hard as rocks.

"Look," Eddie struggles to sit up in the chair. "I didn't mean to put the Doc or you in danger. Wendy needs help. She's in big trouble."

"What kind of trouble?" Frank's still standing over Eddie.

"Something to do with her asshat husband. I didn't even know she was married, that's what kind of idiot I am. She asked to talk to you Doc, or to Pepper. That's why I brought her here. I didn't think we'd be followed."

"Where have you been, Wendy?" I ask. "What's going on?"

"I didn't kill anybody. I swear on Mysti's life." She shakes her head, tears and hair whip around her face.

"Who's following you and why?"

She snorts. Wipes her nose on the heel of her hand. I take her by the shoulders and turn her so that we are face to face. "This is going to stop, right now. You are in deep trouble that's only going to get deeper if you don't start telling me what's going on and how you're involved. Because I know you're involved."

"I'm still sick from the abortion. I need a doctor."

"I'm the only doctor you're going to see for a while. Start talking."

"Why are you being so cruel?"

"I'm trying to figure out what on earth is going on so I can help you."

"Eddie's helping me."

"Eddie is a suspect in two murders, just like you."

She blinks her eyes, grabs my hands. "You have to believe me. I had nothing to do with any of it. I can't go to jail. I need to take care of Mysti. Are you going to arrest me? Do I need a lawyer?"

"I'm not a cop, Wendy. You know that. And you're not under arrest. What I'm saying is that things will go better for you if I'm on your side. And the only way that's going to happen is if you start telling me the truth."

Wendy's eyes flick from me to Eddie and back to me.

"I didn't want Weejay to die. I love him."

She looks at me for a response. Under less pressing circumstances, I would have asked her to define her terms. How naïve do you have to be to love a man who has left you in the lurch, abandoned all responsibility for his child and uses you to save his own skin. Ask me why I love Frank and I can give you a long list of adjectives: funny, intelligent, kind, self-sufficient, reliable, and cares deeply about my well-being. And that's the short list.

"WeeJay's not a bad person. He did a robbery, got busted for using meth and sent to prison before Mysti was born. He's never even met her. At first, I thought he was doing great. He enrolled in a drug program. Then he started writing that he was always afraid, couldn't stand being locked up, felt like he was going crazy. Then he wrote he was feeling better, saying a really powerful person was protecting him. I was happy for that except he started looking dope sick when I visited. I know how he is when he gets like that. He wants to die. Then he started asking me for small favors, little bits of information that he could trade for dope, I said okay, as long as he promised to get back into the program."

"What kind of favors? Did he ask you to delay the fire department from getting to Jerry's trailer? Did he want you to warn Badger's people when the cops were going to raid his massage parlor?"

"Weejay promised Jerry wouldn't get hurt. They only needed a minute or two delay. They just wanted to scare him, make him call 911. Get him in trouble with the cops again. Weejay is my baby's father. I had to help him. If he couldn't pay off his dope debt, he said Badger was going to kill him. He got transferred to Susanville. But Badger's got connections there too. That's why

Weejay took off. That's where I went after the abortion, to meet him in a motel. That's where we were when that girl got killed."

"Where is Weejay now?" She shrugs.

"We only had two nights together. When I woke up yesterday morning, he was gone. That's why Badger is coming after me, to teach Weejay a lesson. That's why Eddie's helping me."

"What about Stell?"

"She threw me out. Said I was nothing but trouble."

"No fool like an old fool, Doc." Eddie flips on a floor lamp. Frank turns it off again. "I mean what the hell else do I have in my life to be proud of? Flipping burgers? Slinging hash? So, I go charging in on my white horse and fuck it all up."

A car cruises past the front of the house, its headlights penetrating through the sheer drapes covering the windows. I hold my breath. The lights disappear down the street. One of the neighbors coming home from work or dinner out.

I can see the whites of Eddie's eyes in the dim light. "Fucking Badger is after me. Hates my guts."

"Just a neighbor, Eddie. Nothing to be alarmed about."

Another set of headlights crawl across the window, this time coming from the opposite direction. A neighbor going out to pick up a pizza or collect a child from band practice. The car stops. I hear four doors opening and the dull thud as they close. Frank grabs a log from the fireplace, holds it in his hand like a bat and moves toward the telephone. A light beam plays over the window. I hear footsteps and the crunch of breaking shrubbery. Eddie rolls forward out of his chair onto the carpet. Wendy sits like an ice statue, frozen in fear. Someone hammers on the front door. Five hard knocks with the head of something hard. Like a flashlight.

"Police. Open up."

Frank signals me to stay put. I ignore him and walk to the

door, sideways like a crab, hoping to offer less of a target. Frank follows holding the log.

"Identify yourself," I say, using my outside voice.

"I can't until you open the door."

I reach for the doorknob. Pepper and Tom in police jackets with two uniformed officers are standing like Christmas carolers on our front step.

"Sorry about the bushes," Tom says as he walks in. Eddie rolls over and groans. "Look who we have here. Bonnie and Clyde."

Pepper walks over to Wendy and lifts her by the arm. "Not to worry, Wendy, I'll tell you who Bonnie and Clyde are when we get to the station."

Tom pulls Eddie to his feet and ties his hands behind his back with plastic cuffs. "Got anything you want to say, old man?"

"Badger's gangbangers. They were following us. They are after me, 'cause I'm the one that put Badger away. They'll be back. Doc and her boyfriend need protection."

Pepper turns from the door. One hand on Wendy's shoulder. "There are no gangbangers, Eddie. Tom and I are the ones who've been following you in an unmarked car we borrowed from another department. It's got tinted windows, just like the bad guys."

Frank and I watch them leave, Eddie and Wendy in handcuffs, their heads bent to the ground. A real-life perp-walk across our front lawn. Clusters of wide-eyed neighbors gather to watch the ragged parade. Things like this don't happen here.

"Everything's okay." Frank waves at the neighbors. "Nothing to worry about. Everything's under control." He takes my arm and steers me back into the house. As soon as we're inside, he pours himself a tumbler of bourbon. I start to pour myself a glass of pinot noir and stop because I have to go to headquarters to help sort out this mess.

“Never again,” Frank says.

“Never again what?”

“Do you put yourself or me in danger.”

“I didn’t know they were coming. They’ve been missing for days. Nobody knew where they were. You saw for yourself. Eddie forced himself in. I didn’t tell him or Wendy they could use our house to hide in.”

“I know you Dot. When it comes to work you have no boundaries. Your clients can call you morning, noon, or night. You’re always available. Whenever and wherever. If I want your attention, I have to get in line.” He takes a swig of whiskey. “Or commit a crime.”

34

There's a throng of reporters hovering around the gate to the employee parking lot at headquarters. Their shouted questions follow me in the dark as I walk from my car to the back door. The news that two KPD employees involved in a double murder were arrested at my house has turned me into a celebrity and a confederate. Was I helping the suspects, someone shouts? Hiding them in my house? Aiding their planned escape? I feel like I'm being stoned in the public square by a herd of morons who expect me to publicly confess my sins.

The quiet inside headquarters is even worse—a mix of shock and shame that has settled over everyone like a poisonous smog. One breach of the public trust is all it takes to cast a shadow over every law enforcement professional in the country. Inflaming the media. Energizing anti-police protesters. Causing police families to hide in their houses to avoid a public pummeling from friends, teachers, and neighbors. Whatever Eddie and Wendy have or haven't done, they've made everyone's job harder. Mine included.

Pepper and Tom are in the break room. There's a tray of sandwiches and a carafe of coffee on the table in front of them. Tom's head is tipped back against his chair. Pepper is leaning on the table, eyes closed, her head on her arms like a schoolgirl during nap time.

"I see Fran's been here," I say. "At least you don't have to drink vile coffee and eat cold baloney sandwiches from the vending machine."

Tom lifts his head. "She was concerned about Eddie. We were an afterthought."

Pence opens the door. He's dressed for the media in a suit with creases so sharp I could file my nails on them. And a mood to match. "Whaddya got? And why is she here?"

I don't have to ask who *she* is.

"You cannot involve the doctor in your interviews with Eddie and Wendy. They were hiding in her house. She's a person of interest, same as they are."

"I was not hiding them. They forced their way in. I didn't invite them. I didn't even know they were coming."

The corners of Pence's mouth turn into an upside-down crescent. "With all due respect, Doctor, I'm taking nothing you say at face value."

Pepper stands. "Eddie swears that he had nothing to do with anything. He was only helping Wendy because she's in trouble; he didn't even know how much trouble until he heard Wendy talking to the Doc about her husband."

"Eddie loves being a cop," I say. "He wouldn't do anything to put his fellow officers in danger."

Tom's face flushes. "The hell he wouldn't. Eddie Rimbauer sucked at being a cop. Showed up for work hungover, spent half his shifts crapped out in the back of his patrol car, sleeping under a bridge."

"Officer Rutgers," Pence is in command-presence mode. "Two, possibly three of my employees may be involved in a double murder." He looks at me. "I am interested in Rimbauer's current actions, not his past performance. What is he saying about the murders?"

"Zippo. He refuses to be in the same room with me. Won't talk to anyone but the Doc. I told him I'd pass that on. Your call, chief."

"The doctor is, as I said, a person of interest. In addition to which she has no training in interrogation. She is not qualified to interview suspects. Do I make myself clear?"

Pence turns to Pepper. "What are you hearing from our dispatcher?"

"She talks a lot but says nothing. She's our leak. She's already admitted as much to the Doc, but she's playing innocent about the two murders. Says anything she did she did to help her husband. If I push her any harder, she'll lawyer up."

The door to the break room opens. Raylene walks in. "Sorry to interrupt. We've just had a call from Bradenton Prison. Willard Joy has been arrested near Lakeville, hitch-hiking alone, heading north toward the Oregon border. Officers notified Susanville who notified Bradenton who remembered we were inquiring about his whereabouts. According to the Lakeville police, Mr. Joy is eager to trade information about Badger in exchange for a guarantee that he be transferred to an out-of-state prison and held in a special housing unit for his own protection."

"I'm on it." Pepper jumps to her feet.

"Me too. Lakeville, here we come," Tom heads for the door.

"Wait a minute, wait a minute." Pence stands. "You can't both go. I need one of you here."

"Send me," Pepper steps forward. "Tom alienates people. Weejay is our only link between Wendy and Badger. We can't afford to piss him off."

"Go," Pence says before Tom has a chance to defend himself.

"Call Lakeville PD for me, please, Raylene." Pepper starts to leave, a tiny smirk on her lips. “I’m going to run home, pack a bag, take a shower. The drive between here and Lakeville is about four hours, just enough time for Mr. Willard Weejay Joy to appreciate the accommodations. I should be at Lakeville PD by sunrise.” She turns back to Tom. “Not to worry, Buddy. I got this.”

35

Early morning is usually peaceful. Frank leaves for work at six-thirty and I have thirty minutes, sometimes a whole hour, to myself. Just me, my coffee, the morning paper, and the irritating sound of my cell phone.

"Have you heard from Pepper?" It's Raylene. She doesn't have to identify herself. I'd know her silken alto voice anywhere.

"No." I look at my watch. "She's probably still at Lakeville PD and Willard Joy is crying for mercy. Confessing to everything from killing Pixie to kidnapping the Lindbergh baby."

"According to the Lakeville Police, Pepper never showed up."

My stomach drops. "Say that again, please."

"The Lakeville Police called us, wanting to know why Pepper hadn't shown up yet."

"Has anyone checked her apartment?"

"That's the first thing Pence did. She's not there. And she's not answering her cell phone. Tom hasn't heard from her either. The chief thinks Badger is protecting his assets."

I get in my car and head for headquarters. I'm shaking, inside and out. Pence is wrong. Badger isn't protecting Weejay. It's as Pepper predicted. He's trying to force me to find his son. I pull up in front of headquarters and turn around the minute

I see Pence standing on the front steps talking to a gaggle of reporters. There's a smaller group off to the side, talking to the public information officer. The entire building is ringed by television trucks. No way I'm going to get into the employee parking lot without being mobbed. I need a place to think. To hide. I take a deep breath and drive to Fran's nearly empty, post-breakfast, pre-lunch cafe. I'm not worried about running into anyone from the department. The usual gaggle of coffee-drinking KPD officers will be out looking for Pepper.

Fran is sitting at her own counter, staring at a coffee-stained newspaper and a plate of scrambled eggs. "Better eat your eggs before they get cold."

"They've been cold for at least ten minutes." She swivels on her stool.

"What can I get you, Dot?"

"Sit, sit. I'll get my own." I walk around the counter, pour myself a cup of coffee and sit next to her.

"Eddie didn't do this murder." She stubs her index finger on the newspaper headline in cadence with every word. "He's not capable of killing anyone but himself."

"I know that."

"He's a fool, that's what he is. Falling for that little—I won't say what I think she is. Like someone said, God gave man enough blood to run his brain and his penis, just not at the same time." She crosses herself and mutters something under her breath. "This is the most trouble he's ever been in. And he did it stone cold sober. I give up. Nothing changes. He never gets it right."

She stands and starts wiping the counter with a damp cloth. Over and over she rubs at an invisible stain as though trying to rub out a cache of bad memories. I put my hand on hers. "It's spotless Fran, sit down. Please."

She puts her hands on her hips but doesn't move. "I suppose

I should be grateful he's in jail. At least I know he's not lying in a ditch drunk or dead."

"I know you're worried about him. I'm worried about him too. But I'm more worried about Pepper."

Before she has a chance to ask what I mean, my cell phone chirps. A text from Frank and another from Raylene. Frank wants to know what time I'll be available for dinner. Raylene tells me to call her ASAP and wants to know when I'll be back at headquarters. Not until the hordes of reporters go away, I tell her the minute she answers the phone.

"Any word about Pepper?"

"None. Hang on a minute. The chief wants to talk to you. I'll transfer."

There's a click and Pence gets on the phone. "Where the hell are you?"

This is so Pence. One minute he literally can't stand the sight of me. The next he's coming unglued because he doesn't know where I am.

"I'm at Fran's. I couldn't face driving through that mob of reporters."

"I've been on the phone with Lakeville PD all morning. No sign of Pepper. Willard Joy has no idea where she is either. Denies Badger has taken Pepper in order to protect him. Just the opposite. He's terrified. Convinced Badger is out to kill him, not help him. Promises to tell the police what he knows, except he doesn't know anything. Keeps swearing that neither he nor Wendy had anything to do with the hooker's murder."

"Her name was Pixie."

"I don't care if her name was Cleopatra, Queen of the Nile. She's dead. On my watch."

He's pacing. I can hear his feet moving, the uptick in his breathing.

"Lakeville PD interrogated Willard for three hours straight and he never changed his story. Insists that he and Wendy were shacked up in some motel when the murder happened and neither one of them had anything to do with the now posthumously respected, Miss Pixie. I have absolutely nothing to tell the press, the Mayor, the FBI, the City Council, or anyone else."

Forget Pixie's battered body and Pepper's disappearance. Tragedy matters only insofar as it threatens Pence's reputation and his on-camera appearance. I want to put my fist through the phone and rip out his shellacked silver hair. I take a long breath. Tap the meridian point over my mythical third eye, hoping the super-trendy tapping technique that is guaranteed to cure everything from insomnia to indigestion, will keep me calm enough to avoid telling Pence to go to hell and lose my job.

"Still there, Meyerhoff?"

"Still here." I take a second breath. Imagine exhaling all my anger. "What are you going to do?"

"Let Lakeville PD deal with Mr. Joy."

"I mean about Pepper."

"Every law enforcement agency in Northern California is looking for her. There's nothing more I can do."

"Why did you call me?"

"Damned if I know," he says and slams down the phone.

Fran is watching me with interest. Pence's voice was so loud she probably heard every word. Before she has a chance to ask the question that's written all over her face, my phone goes off again. I don't recognize the calling number. This is not the time to field robo-calls or listen to a cheerful reminder about my upcoming dental appointment.

The raspy male voice on the other end wants to know who he's talking to.

"What do you mean who am I? You called me. Who are you?"

"I'm looking for Moorehuff. Dr. Moorehuff."

There's a rumble of indistinct voices in the background. A change of hands.

"Doc?" Pepper's voice is quavering at an unnatural pitch.

"Pepper, where are you? Are you safe?"

"I'm in red square."

Somebody snatches the phone and muffles it with his hand. I can hear talking, angry but indistinct. What does she mean, red square? Red Square's in Russia. Pepper can't be in Russia. Then I remember the recording app she put on my phone, the red square with the little white telephone in the middle. I tap it to start recording. She gets back on the phone.

"Find Badger's son. Get him a photograph and an address. He'll let me go if you do."

There's more indistinct conversation. Someone is yelling in the background. Pepper yells back, her hand only partly covering the phone.

"Are you hurt?"

"Don't try to trace this call. If you do . . ." There's a scuffle. Mr. Raspy Voice grabs the phone.

"What your friend is trying to say is if you want to see her again, do what Badger asks. And don't waste time. Some of the boys here are getting antsy. This bitch is quite a challenge." He disconnects.

Fran stares at me. At my shaking hands. Pepper sounded desperate, her voice thin, shrill, almost a whine. Whatever is happening to her and whoever's doing it has pushed her beyond endurance. The Pepper I know would never ask me or anyone else to put themselves in harm's way to protect her. Not unless she had no other choice. I text Frank. I don't want to talk to him directly. I make up a story about forgetting I registered for a class tonight. A required class I need to keep my psychology license. I'm lying, but no way am I going to risk telling him that I'm going to Bradenton Prison to talk to a psychopathic inmate who looks more like a mural than a man. I know what he'll say. All of which will be true but, given Pepper's situation, deeply irrelevant.

By the time I get off the phone, Fran has brought me a bowl of soup and a sourdough roll, slathered in butter.

"Eat," she says. "I don't know what you're up to. Frankly, I'd rather not know. But, whatever it is, it's better not to do it on an empty stomach."

36

I call Pence to tell him about Pepper's phone call and that I'm on my way to Bradenton to talk to Badger. He tells me to turn around. He needs my phone to trace Pepper's call.

Then he changes his mind, says they probably used a burner. He asks if I want an officer to accompany me. I turn him down. Badger wants me. Anyone else will just shut him down. Pence wishes me good luck, tells me to be careful and makes me promise to report back to him as soon as I finish talking to Badger because he has a press briefing scheduled for tonight.

It takes more than an hour to drive to the prison and another hour to get through the damn screening. Doesn't matter that I've been screened before, that I work for KPD or that I'm a harmless looking woman wearing glasses and carrying a briefcase. I need to go through it all over again.

Badger's on the edge of his seat, smiling. The interview room is dank, sour with the previous occupant's sweat. Badger rubs his hands together in anticipation. "I got a kid," he says to the guards. "A boy. He's ten. The Doc here is bringing me his picture. She works for the cops, but she's good people. Real good people." He winks at me. "And I'm grateful to her for a lot of things. Pull up a seat, Doc. Make yourself comfortable."

I stand, holding my briefcase in front of me like a shield. "Where's Pepper? What have you done with her?"

He feigns surprise. Or is it confusion? Hard to decipher with his tattoos.

I put my briefcase down, fumble for my phone and tap the recording app Pepper installed. Her voice ricochets off the walls, shrill and full of fear. "Find Badger's son. Give him what he wants. He'll let me go if you do."

Badger puts his hands to his head, one on either side of the swastika that sits like a third eye in the middle of his forehead. "Idiots. I had no idea they would go this far. I am so sorry. Remember how I said I got devoted followers? They know how much I want to find my son. And they know I was waiting and waiting to hear back from you. I guess they got impatient on my behalf."

I have a burst of adrenaline so intense I could lift off the ground and fly around the room, beak sharpened, claws extended. Why did I think Badger possessed even a shred of humanity? Or truthfulness? Why didn't I listen to Frank? Or Pepper? If I had, maybe she wouldn't be God knows where with God knows who having God knows what done to her. I take a deep breath. Then another and another, trying to beat back my anger.

"You need some water, Doc? You don't look so good."

"The only thing I need is to know where Pepper is."

"Wish I could help. I owe you."

"Owe me for what?"

"Best not to say." He tilts his head toward the officers who look like they're sleeping with their eyes open. "Trust me, I don't forget my friends. Let's see it, the picture you brought."

I dig my nails into my palms. "No Pepper, no photo."

Badger's face rearranges itself, his eyes beady and black as obsidian. He lifts from his chair. The officers wake up. One places his hand on a cannister of pepper spray, the other reaches for his radio. Badger waves them off, sits down again.

"You don't have a picture?"

I dig my nails deeper into my palms. "I've been trying to locate your son and his mother. The Bay Area is a big place. It's not easy to find somebody who doesn't want to be found."

"Check the shelters around Kenilworth. You still got connections, don't you? My ex knows them all. Me and her got into it a lot. Her new name is Charlotte Stebbins. Watch out. She gives as good as she gets. Only on me you never saw the bruises."

"Not until you let Pepper go."

His bangs his fists on the table, rattling the chains around his waist and hands. "I do the negotiations here. Not you."

"Finding your son is going to take time. I'm not a detective. Why don't you ask your devoted followers to find your ex and your son? Let Pepper go and leave me out of it."

"Let me explain something to you, Doc. Much as they love me, my devoted followers would steal the shirt off my back if they had the chance." He clasps his shackled hands together like a pastor or a funeral director, his mood changing as fast as a chameleon changes color. "I'm a businessman. I made a pile of dough. All of it goes to my kid. Not his mother. Not my homies. That's why I need to know where he is so when I die, which in this joint could be any minute, my lawyer knows where to send the money, the pink slips, the deeds. Here's my final offer. You find my son and I'll make sure my guys behave themselves until you do." His voice drops to a hoarse whisper. "And don't send nothing in the mail. They open everything first. Give it to Lenny at the front gate. Big belly, bald. He and I got an arrangement. So, any questions? We got a deal?"

"Absolutely not. No deal. Not until you let Pepper go," I say before I'm drowned out by a chorus of shrieking sirens. The guards pull Badger to his feet. A third guard enters the room and rushes me toward the other door.

"Best I can do," Badger yells over the noise. "Take it or leave it."

I shake all the way home. The lockdown, or whatever they call it, took less time to resolve than it took my heart to stop beating a million miles a minute. The guard who locked me in an office for my own safety was so alarmed at my agitation that he insisted on calling a medic to check me out before he let me drive home. I negotiated for a cup of tea instead, just to reassure him I wasn't going to croak on his watch. It wasn't the yelling, the running, the shouts, or the sirens that frightened me. It was Badger's bargain. His son for Pepper's release. I have accomplished nothing. I'm an idiot. How did I ever think the boy I once knew could overcome a horrible start in life and make his way in the world unscathed, his humanity intact? For all I know, that funny little guy with all his endearing quirkiness, was playing me then, just like he's playing me now. Pepper was right. No way either of us can outwit a born psychopath who will stop at nothing to get what he wants.

I check my phone. There are six messages from Pence asking what's happening. No messages from Pepper or her abductors. I call back and get Pence's voice mail. "Sorry, Chief. Nothing to report. You were right about one thing. I am in over my head."

Across the Golden Gate bridge, the zipper divider, a moveable median barrier that separates north from south bound traffic, is doing its job keeping the opposing lanes of commuters from crashing into each other, head-on. Traffic in my direction is mercifully light. By the time I get home the sky is pitch black and Frank is asleep in front of the TV. He wakes up when I open the front door.

"Tough class?"

I fuss around, hang up my coat, pour myself a class of wine for liquid courage. "I didn't go to class, I went to see Badger." Frank sits upright. "Badger's thugs kidnapped Pepper. He's trying to force me to find his son and won't tell me where she is or guarantee her safety unless I do what he wants."

Frank sits me on the couch, his hands on my shoulders. "Slow down. Start again."

It takes me five minutes to get out the whole story. How scared Pepper sounded on the phone. How guilty I feel for not listening to her warnings.

"You didn't listen to me either when I warned you. And you lied to me. Made up a bullshit story about having to go to class. Why couldn't you tell me where you were going? Am I that scary that you have to hide the truth because you think I'll get mad? What are you, a child?" He pushes himself to standing and goes into the kitchen. I can hear him emptying the dishwasher. Muttering to himself. Putting things away with such force I'm sure he'll break all the plates and glasses.

37

First thing in the morning I call Laurie Bender. Laurie is a social worker friend I met in grad school when I interned at the homeless shelter. She's now heading a service organization for battered women. If anyone can help me find Badger's ex-wife and son, it will be her. Pepper needs a lucky break. So do I.

"Charlotte Stebbins? She's one of our successes. Been with us for nearly ten years, moving through the shelter system from board and care to transitional housing. Now she has her own apartment, volunteers at the shelter and is close to finishing her bachelor's degree in social work. She's one of the most determined women I have ever met. Why are you looking for her?"

I explain the situation. Rather than give me any more information, Laurie offers her office as a place to meet this afternoon. On one condition—that she be present.

Laurie's office is on the second floor of a four-story office building next to what was once a church but is now a community center. There are no women sheltered in this location, just administrative offices. No signs, no office register, nothing to entice an angry, abusive husband to force his way in looking for information about his wife's hiding place. Laurie is waiting for me on the sidewalk. She looks to her left and right before unlocking the entry door and heading up the stairs. Her office is anything but plain. The walls are painted in primary colors and covered with posters and paintings. Except for Laurie's large office desk, the furniture is soft and homey. Handmade quilts from the Ladies Auxiliary of a nearby church are draped over the backs of chairs and couches. Butterfly mobiles swing from the ceiling.

Charlotte Stebbins is right on time. She is shorter than I am with curly close cropped light brown hair and pale green eyes. Casually dressed in jeans and a loose-fitting black sweatshirt. Laurie introduces us. Gives a few short facts about how we've known each other for a long time. I extend my hand. Charlotte ignores it and sits, arms folded over her chest, her eyes looking everywhere but in my direction.

"Ms. Stebbins," I say. "Thank you so much for meeting with me. I wouldn't have troubled you unless I really needed your help. I'll get right to the point. Your ex-husband is conducting a large criminal operation from his prison cell, selling dope and running prostitutes. We believe he's responsible for two deaths, that of a wheelchair bound man who died in an arson fire and a young woman who was working as a police informant.

"Most importantly and urgently, the reason I'm here today is that a police officer investigating the death of that informant is missing. We believe your ex has engineered her disappearance."

She shakes her head and pulls a pendant from underneath her shirt. "The man has no limits. The cops gave this to me. It's a panic button. All I have to do is press it and they know where I am. That's how bad he is. I have to wear this for the rest of my life in case he breaks out of prison."

"That's not going to happen," Laurie says.

"You don't know Badger."

Laurie places a reassuring hand on Charlotte's shoulder. "They have enough charges on him for three lifetimes, all of them because of what he did to you."

Charlotte looks directly at my face. Her eyes are steady and defiant. "What has this got to do with me?"

"Your ex has promised to release the missing officer in exchange for two things, a photo of your son and an address." Charlotte stiffens. Rigid lines form around her face and neck. "He wants the address so that, on his death, he can leave your son what he claims is a large amount of money. He seems to think he's going to get murdered in prison."

"That's why you're here? Listen lady, I don't know what Badger told you, but I'm not for sale. Neither is my son. When I was pregnant, that man beat me with his fists, with a motorcycle chain, a broom handle. Anything he could get his hands on. He's never seen my boy. And never will. End of subject."

"I don't mean to insult you. I'm worried about my friend. I don't know what else to do. Who else to ask. I'm afraid he's going to have her killed." I tear up and turn my head away but not before Charlotte sees my face. She turns to Laurie.

"What the hell? What are you getting me into, Laurie? I'd do anything you asked but not this, not when it comes to my son."

"Our relationship doesn't matter, Charlotte. You need to do what's right for you and your son."

"I don't want Badger's money. His money is dirty. I know how he earned it." She shifts in her seat. Rearranges herself to face me again. "I've heard this a million times. Badger was always bragging about how much money he made selling dope and running girls. He lied more than he told the truth. Told me 90 percent of the money he made was going into a trust fund for his son. His son, not our son, his."

"What does he have to gain by lying?" Laurie asks.

"My address. Once he finds out where I am, he's going to send his gang after me and my boy. I won't have that. No way."

Now I see the fear in her face. Hear the quake in her voice. "This is how he is. Thinks money is everything. Beat me almost to death and thought he could make it right by buying me a new car. He doesn't know anything about love or loyalty and calls those gutter rats, always sniffing around him looking for a hand-out, his devoted followers. They talk trash about him. The minute he turns his back they'd take whatever he owned. Including me."

"What if you rent a P.O. box address and I give Badger a picture of somebody else's child? An old photo of someone who's grown up. Or dead. We could send somebody to pick up the money at the post office. That way your son would still get the money and Badger wouldn't know where you are."

"Not going to happen. You don't know Badger. I've been looking over my shoulder for too long. There's not enough money in the world to buy me peace of mind. I'm getting my life together. Finally. That SOB isn't going to stop me, not for a million dollars." She stands. "Come with me."

We walk to the end of the hallway outside Laurie's office and stand at a window overlooking a small courtyard. A young boy, dressed in jeans and a windbreaker, is sitting on a bench absorbed in a book. His hair is light brown and curly, like his mother's.

"That's Jake. He's a good boy. Quiet. Studious. The school thinks he's bright. He's my whole world. Everything I do, I do for him."

"What does he know about his father?"

"He thinks his father is dead. Died in a motorcycle accident. I'm going to have to tell him the truth one day, just not yet. I want to do it when he's mature enough. And when there's a therapist around to help him figure out how he feels. Not just about his father, but about me lying to him for so many years. I hate that I have to lie." Her eyes glisten like green lights in a shallow pool. "I didn't have a choice. Like you said, Badger's in prison but he's still running the streets. As soon as I finish my degree, we're out of here. Going somewhere far away." She looks out the window. Jake waves. Smiles. His eyes are dark like his father's. Charlotte waves back.

"If you don't mind my saying, you're an unlikely pair, you and Badger."

"I don't mind you saying that." She smiles for the first time. "It's a compliment. We are an unlikely pair. I was a rebellious teenager. Drinking. Smoking weed. Cutting school. Badger was a sexy bad boy. My parents were church crazy. Always preaching at me. Being with him was like giving them the finger. It was a wild ride for a time. When I got pregnant, everything changed. I wasn't fun anymore. I wouldn't drink or smoke dope or party with his friends." She puts her hand up. "Wait here a minute."

She leaves by an exit door, her footsteps echoing in the stairwell. A minute later she pops into the courtyard, sits with her arm around Jake's shoulder. Jake points at something on the page and reads aloud. Charlotte whispers in his ear. He looks up. Waves at me. Then they walk up the stairs, back into Laurie's office.

"Hello, Jake," I say. "I'm Dr. Dot Meyerhoff. But everybody calls me Doc." Jake's eyes are bright, alive, curious. "I'm a psychologist. Do you know what that is?"

"There's one at my school. She teaches us how to relax and not be angry or scared. Are you going to teach my mom too?"

Charlotte laughs, tells Jake it's time for them to go. They hug Laurie goodbye and wave at me as they leave. Charlotte stops short of the door. "I hope you find your friend soon, Dr.

Meyerhoff and that she's okay. But watch your step. Badger's not stupid. The last thing you want to do is piss him off."

As soon as she goes, Laurie turns to me, her face twisted in anger. "This was a mistake. I'm sorry I ever agreed to it. Don't pretend this is an even exchange, your officer for information about Jake. It's not even close. Jake is an innocent child. Your officer is an adult. She knew police work was dangerous when she hired on. No one forced her into the job. She knew what to expect."

I want to argue, tell her that it doesn't make any difference what Pepper believed about herself when she was a rookie. Every cop I've ever counseled whose life was threatened—or had been in a fight for survival—never felt the way they once expected to feel: brave, competent, and in control. Never.

38

The air is cold by the time I get home from Laurie's office, the sky etched with blood red streaks. Frank greets me at the door with a question, "Any word from Pepper?" I shake my head, take off my coat, slip out of my shoes. Frank pours me a glass of wine. It's one of the things I love most about him. He doesn't harbor a grudge. Despite our cross words last night, he looks truly happy to see me.

"How was your day?" I ask.

"Come on, Dot. You don't want to know about my day. Tell me what's going on. You must be frantic."

I tell him about Charlotte. How much I liked her and her son. How dangerous it would be to believe Badger meant them no harm. Even if what he said about leaving his son money was true, the money would come at too great a price. I think about Pixie, how she might still be alive if her mother had protected her the way Charlotte is protecting Jake.

"I tried everything I could think of. I told Charlotte we could use a picture of somebody else's long dead child who lives in Timbuktu. She wouldn't go for it. Too scared. And with reason. For all I know she and Jake boarded a plane to Iceland the minute they left Laurie's office. I don't have any other options, except what Pence is always telling me to do, leave policework to the cops."

"Actually, that's not a bad idea."

"Leaving policework to the cops?"

He raises his eyebrows, splays his hands. "Giving Badger a phony photo. Who are you living with, Dot? What have I been doing for years? Photography. P-h-o-t-o-g-r-a-p-h-y. Remember when you begged me to fix your chin for the photo on your book jacket? How do you think I did that? Photoshop. All I need is a picture of Badger as a kid and I can put something together. It will have enough likeness to him that he'll never know it isn't his son."

"I don't understand. You never want to get involved with my work."

"I don't. Under ordinary circumstances. But these circumstances are hardly ordinary, are they? It's a case of enlightened self-interest. I know you. I don't want to live with a crazy woman. And that's what you'll be until Pepper gets released."

"If she gets released," I say.

"See what I mean. You're already in catastrophe mode."

"And you aren't?"

"No. I'm not as close to Pepper as you are and there's no way anything I did or didn't do is responsible for her disappearance. I don't have that on my conscience. You do. The sooner Pepper gets back, the sooner you'll settle down. And the sooner you settle down, the sooner we can get back to planning our wedding. If it will speed things up, I'm all in."

"Badger will never believe it. He'll know the picture is a phony."

"People see what they want to see. Believe what they want to believe. Ask anybody in the advertising industry. Badger's primed. He wants a picture of his kid so badly, he'd accept anything you give him."

***

I do a Google search for Badger and get four hits. The first is a photo of a grinning younger Lieutenant Jay Pence announcing Badger's conviction for running a prostitution ring in the Mateo Park Trailer Court. Streaks of white starting to stipple his black hair. The second is a ten-year-old booking photo of Badger covered in tattoos. The third shows Eddie receiving a medal for bravery after subduing the notorious Badger in a gun fight. The fourth, the picture I had hoped to find, is a grainy head shot of a sullen, skinny thirteen-year-old Badger, peach fuzz on clear skin, making headlines as one of the youngest people ever remanded to juvenile court for selling drugs.

Frank stares at the photo. Moves it around with his index finger while I look over his shoulder.

"Give him green eyes like Charlotte and black hair, like Badger. He'd be wearing a collared white shirt like a school uniform. And a different background, a park or some anonymous building. No identifying landmarks. And short hair. Charlotte would never let Jake grow his hair that long. It needs to be perfect, Frank. There's too much at stake."

Frank disappears into his study. I talk to Raylene three times. Still nothing from Pepper or Tom or the hundreds of cops who are out looking for her. I turn the news on and off. The smiling photos of Pepper as a rookie, Pepper at the police Olympics, Pepper getting a commendation for starting a girl's midnight basketball team, make me cry. Somewhere around midnight, Frank, looking tired but happy, shakes me awake. I've fallen asleep on the couch. He hands me a photoshopped likeness so realistic that Badger could have sat for it himself when he was a kid. With just enough Charlotte in his face to be convincing.

"Here you go," Frank says. "Put it in the mail. First thing in the morning."

"Mail takes seven days, Frank. Sometimes more. Prison rules mean all mail has to be inspected." I take Frank's arm. "I won't stay long. I'll just hand him the photo and leave. The guards can inspect it on the spot."

"No way." He snatches the photo out of my hands. "This is my masterpiece. If anyone's going to deliver it, I am. In person. Non-negotiable. Or else." He makes a motion to tear the photo in two.

"Stop." I put my hands out. "They won't let you in to see Badger. You're not on the approved visitors list. Ask for Lenny at the front gate. Big belly, bald. He and Badger have an arrangement."

39

Frank is gone before sunrise. No goodbye kiss, no note on the kitchen table. Two and a half hours later, he texts me. *Mission Accomplished.*

It's a nippy day; a brisk wind is whipping the fallen leaves into tiny tornadoes. I open the front door to collect the newspaper and walk smack into an arrangement of red and pink gladiolas big enough for a state sponsored funeral. A neighbor drives past, honks her horn and mouths the word beautiful. I lug the flowers inside. The attached note tells me to prepare for a pleasant surprise. It's signed with two hand drawn smiley faces connected by an ampersand, the larger of the two faces covered in tattoo-like squiggles. I throw everything in the trash bin and leave for headquarters. Eddie is in the hall, outside my office.

"I thought you were in jail. What are you doing here?"

"Skipping through flowers and farting rainbows." He tears a soft sugared donut in half and stuffs both halves in his mouth. The door to the police garage opens releasing a cold draft. Eddie slams his meaty palm down on a stack of paper napkins to stop them from blowing away. Pence walks in, wearing a tweed overcoat, a wool muffler and carrying a briefcase that probably cost more than a plane ticket to Europe.

"Morning, Chief," Eddie says. "Coffee on the house."

Pence walks past him without a word and stands at my door. "In your office, Doctor. Now."

Eddie stares at Pence's back, not even trying to conceal his hurt. "Twenty years in this fucking joint and all I am is the fuzz that was."

"Any word from Pepper?" Pence and I practically step on each other's words. Neither one of us wants to say what not hearing from her or about her might mean.

"You released Eddie. I'm surprised."

"If we had laws criminalizing idiots, he'd be facing a life sentence. I tell you this, Eddie's no match for Wendy. She's really something. Wouldn't talk until I told her the D.A. was going to charge her as an accessory to Jerry's murder. Swore she had nothing to do with Jerry's death, but she did have information to share that might help us solve his murder." He pauses for dramatic effect. "Wendy thinks Stell was involved because Stell rescued Jerry's dog the day before the fire proving she knew what was going to happen. If Stell didn't light the match herself, then she must have looked the other way."

I remember Pepper's prediction. That Wendy would throw Stell under the bus in a hot minute if it meant saving her own skin. Pepper lives in a black and white world, secure in her own opinions. My world is full of nuance, theory, and supposition. Wendy's both a victim and perpetrator, not one or the other. Badger's the same, part crook, part consequence of a lousy start in life.

"I don't know what she was expecting, but the minute I informed her there could be two accessories to one crime, she turned on the waterworks. Started playing the victim, begged me to believe it was her husband who told her to keep Jerry on the phone. He promised her no one would be hurt. I had to understand that she always did what her husband told her to do to save him from being killed by Badger. But now that Weejay was safely in custody and Badger can't get to him, she'll tell me anything I want to know. Whatever she did, she only did to save her husband. And here's the corker. She really loves working for KPD and hopes she could have her job back after this is all over. What a performance."

Pence leans against my desk, drained from his own breathless oratory.

"She is a world class con artist. How did you miss this, Dr. Meyerhoff?"

He only calls me Dr. Meyerhoff when he's angry.

"Are you implying this is my fault? May I remind you that I only met Wendy for the first time the night of the fire. Reason being, you don't think it's necessary to subject dispatchers to pre-employment psychological screening because they don't carry guns." This appears to be news to him. "At least you got Wendy to confess to warning the massage parlors about the raids."

He smiles, thanks me, and says it was no big thing, he was only doing his job, happy he hadn't lost his detective chops. I resist the impulse to throw him out of my office.

"So, when you asked her if she knows where Pepper is, what did she say?"

The color drains from his face. He stands up, briefcase in hand. "I was just about to ask, but when she saw I wasn't falling for her tricks, she clammed up, wouldn't say another word. Said the only person she would talk to is you." He turns at the door. "Be clear about this, Dr. Meyerhoff, anything she says, and I mean anything, comes back to me. ASAP."

40

The interview room at the county detention center is painted institutional green. Flecks of unknown substances stain the wall. I try not to touch anything. There's a small metal table and two metal chairs. A video camera grinds away in the corner of the ceiling like a great eye in the sky. Wendy's lost weight. She looks worse than she did after the abortion. Her once porcelain smooth skin is faded to a greenish gray. Her beautiful hair falls in oily strings over the baggy jail-issued orange jumpsuit.

"Get me out of here. Please." She starts crying the minute she sees me. "I need to see Mysti. My mother refuses to bring her to see me. Won't even visit me herself. Says I'm where I belong." She swipes her face with the back of her hands. "I was only trying to help Weejay. I'm sorry for what I did. You have to believe me, everything I did, I did for him. Not for money, not for anything but him. Because I love him. He loves me."

This last, almost a wail.

"Your husband may have needed you, Wendy, but he doesn't love you. He was using you to save his own neck. Your husband abandoned you. Ran off. Left you in a motel, sick as you were, to fend for yourself. Is that your definition of love?" Her lips scrunch into a pout. I'm telling her the truth and she doesn't like hearing it. "Do you know anything at all about Pepper's disappearance?"

"Pepper's disappeared?" Her eyes snap into focus. "When? I've been locked up here for days. I didn't know." She watches me watch her. "Seriously, I don't know where she is. Until you just said, I didn't even know she was missing." She flaps her hands like she's trying to fly.

"You're in very serious trouble, Wendy. You are an accessory to one, maybe two, murders. You are going to prison. Your only chance to negotiate for a better deal is to tell me everything you know."

"I have. I will. Cross my heart."

"What about Pixie, Pepper's confidential informant? The dead woman by the creek."

She puts her hand over her mouth. Shakes her head, dragging her oily locks across her shoulders. "Me and Weejay had nothing to do with her. Nothing. You have to believe me." I stand up. Start to put on my coat. "Where are you going?"

"I don't have time for this Wendy. You know more than you're saying and you're foolish not to tell me. It's in your own best interest." I lean over, my hands flat on the table. "It's time for you to grow up. Stop pretending Weejay is going to take care of you and start taking care of yourself." I button my coat. Slowly.

"What kind of better deal?"

"A shorter sentence. Prison closer to home so you can get visitors. A minimum detention facility. Maybe a prison where women inmates are allowed to spend time with their children."

Wendy raises her eyebrows. "There are prisons like that?"

"Keeping inmate mothers in touch with their children prevents recidivism, it keeps their kids in school and has lots of other benefits. I know how much you love Mysti. You're a good mother. I'll go to bat for you, but only if you tell me everything you know."

"I told you. I don't know where Pepper is."

I sit down again. "What about Pixie? Did you know she was Pepper's confidential informant?"

Wendy shakes her head. "I knew about her. I never met her."

"How did you know about her? That's restricted information."

"I can't remember." I head for the door. "Tom." Her voice is barely above a whisper. "Tom Rutgers told me right after I came back to work. He likes to hang around dispatch, flirt with the girls. I think he was trying to impress me. Telling me he thought it was a waste for Pepper to hire a CI. That CIs can't be counted on. They lie. It was just a casual remark. I thought maybe it wasn't even true because Tom likes to brag about what a good cop he is. How everybody else is stupid."

"And after Tom told you, you told Badger?"

She nods her head. "That was our deal. Anytime I learned anything related to Badger, I was supposed to tell Weejay and he would tell Badger. But Weejay didn't have phone privileges that week, so I called Badger direct. I didn't see the harm. I thought Badger would just get mad, or like Tom said, pay her to lie to Pepper. If I had known she was going to get killed, I would never had said anything. You'll help me, Doctor, won't you? I've told you everything I know."

"Everything? Are you sure?"

"Absolutely," she says, making the mark of the cross over her heart.

41

Pepper is back! I don't know whether to cry, yell, or set off fireworks. I call Frank and babble into his voice mail. "You're my hero. It was the photo that did it. You're genius. Thank you, thank you, thank you. I am so relieved. Everyone at headquarters is cheering. Fist bumping, high fiving. Dinner on me. Champagne, steak, kinky sex, whatever you want."

Raylene grabs me in a warm, moist hug. I can tell she's been crying. Fran sends Eddie over with a sheet cake big enough to feed the entire department. Pence is beaming in front of the TV cameras, as though he had just won the police chiefs' MVP award. He plucks the reporters' questions out of the air like he's catching hummingbirds on the fly.

"When can we talk to Officer Hunt?" someone shouts.

"In a day or two. Officer Hunt would be back at work now if it wasn't for me putting my foot down. She's a dedicated officer. Doesn't want to take any time off. She's not badly hurt. Nothing to worry about. Even so, I'm insisting she stay home, no visitors, until she has a clean bill of health from her doctor."

Another shout, as much a demand as a question. "What happened to her?"

"Officer Hunt has been working tirelessly, back-to-back

shifts, in her pursuit of the individuals responsible for the two recent murders. There will be a thorough investigation. What I can tell you is that she was on her way to interview a person of interest who is in custody at the Lakeville Police Department when she had a vehicle accident. Lucky for her, and for us, she wasn't killed."

Pepper looks terrible. There's a huge purplish knot on her head. Her upper lip is swollen pulling her mouth to one side. She has a chipped front tooth and a deep gash on her chin.

"No visitors. Pence was supposed to tell everyone." She checks the street with a sweep of her eyes, pulls me inside her apartment without a word, double locks the door and limps to the couch. There's a half-finished beer on the coffee table.

"I'm so glad to see you. I've been frantic. We've all been frantic." I reach out to hug her and she draws back, both hands raised in front of her chest. Not a gesture of surrender, but one of self-protection.

"Sorry. I think I got a couple of bruised ribs. Hugging hurts." She sits, grimacing with the effort. I move a pile of books off a leather hassock and pull up next to her.

"Want a beer?" she says.

It's way too early for alcohol but given what I imagine Pepper's been through, I don't say anything.

"Have you seen a doctor? Maybe your ribs are broken, not bruised."

She shakes her head. "I'm fine."

"You don't look fine."

"What a doofus. Fell asleep on my way to Lakeville. Crashed my car. Knocked myself out. Lucky I'm alive. Good story, huh?" She gives me a lopsided smile. "It will be in all the papers. Officer Hunt survives near fatal line-of-duty crash. Badger and his flunkies will think I'm keeping my mouth shut, like they told me. They'll think different when I nail their sorry asses to the wall." She takes a swig of beer and flinches. "Shit. That hurt."

She's slurring her words. I can't tell if it's her swollen lip or the beer. She covers her mouth with her swollen hand. Her knuckles are scraped raw. I can only imagine why. Or how.

"Maybe lighten up on the beer a little?" I say. "Alcohol isn't the best choice for now. Not while your body is pumping out stress hormones." She puts the bottle down.

"You don't think I'm fooling anyone with that story?"

"I doubt it. I went to the press briefing. Reporters are already asking questions. There will be an investigation. Just to be clear, if anyone asks me if I know what happened to you, I'm not going to lie."

"You don't know what happened to me."

"Badger had you kidnapped. You called me on the phone. Remember?" She picks up her beer, looks at it like she'd never seen it before, and puts it down again.

"Why didn't you tell me about his son?"

"I did. Right after we met him for the first time at Bradenton." I'm starting to worry she has a concussion or a TBI.

"Why didn't you tell me he kept pressuring you? I could have played him. Set him up. Done a sting. Instead, there I was, fat, dumb, and happy. Cruising along, listening to the radio, when those assholes ran me off the road."

Without warning, she starts to hyperventilate. The residual layer of beer foam on her lips makes her look as though she's frothing at the mouth. Her body is reacting to the memory as if she is, once again, under attack. I move next to her on the couch.

"Deep breaths," I say, keeping my voice firm but gentle. "Short breath in, long breath out. I'm going to put my hand on your shoulder now. Okay?" She doesn't respond, her eyes are fixed, staring. I lower my hand gently. "You're safe, Pepper. You're in your apartment. The door is locked. No one can get in. Keep breathing, short breath in, long breath out. You're sitting on the couch, remember? Feel your back against the pillows. Feel your feet on the floor." Her breathing slows. "Can you feel my hand on your shoulder?" She nods. "Do you remember what you are wearing?" She pulls at the hem of her sweatshirt to check the color, then curls up against the arm of the couch.

"Give me ten, Doc. I need to close my eyes."

A few motionless minutes pass before she falls asleep. She's exhausted, maybe a little drunk and surely rebounding from all the adrenaline her body has been putting out. I cover her with a blanket I find folded across the foot of her bed and listen to her snore.

I look around. Her living room, like her bedroom, is impersonal. No plants, no tchotchkes, no antiques. Only a few family pictures on top of the TV cabinet. The furniture is blond wood with honey colored upholstery offset by a brightly patterned area rug with matching throw pillows. I recognize the style. Online shopping. Rent-to-own. Just like Pepper, engaging but anonymous. I'm struck by how little I know her.

Twenty minutes pass. She wakes with a loud gasp. Looks around the room in a panic. She sees me sitting in a chair. "Holy shit. For a minute, I didn't know where I was."

"You're at home, safe in your own apartment," I say.

Her breath slows like a steam train pulling into the station. She swings her legs over the couch and sits up, her head in her hands. I count to twenty before offering to get her a glass of water. By the time I return she's leaning back, her legs propped against the edge of the coffee table. She upends the entire glass in one long swallow and closes her eyes, the glass still in her hand.

"Want to know how it happened?" She is talking to me with her eyes still closed.

"It's okay Pepper, you don't have to talk about it now. Get some more sleep, some food. Then maybe see a doctor. We can talk when you're rested."

"They forced me off the road. I didn't see them coming until they were next to me. There were four of them. Dragged me out of the car, kicking and hitting, took my gun and threatened to kill me with it or shove it . . ." She chokes at the memory. "Goddamnit! I let them take my gun."

"You didn't let them take your gun, Pepper, you were ambushed. Outnumbered. Four of them, one of you. You didn't have any options."

"I should have shot the fuckers. All of them." She sits forward, throws off the blanket. "I need to go to Lakeville and interview Willard Joy before one of Badger's guys kills him to shut him up."

"The Lakeville deputies interviewed him for hours. He never changed his story. Swears he and Wendy had nothing to do with Pixie's death."

"Lakeville S.O? Freaking bunch of farm boys. They don't know what they're doing."

"You're in no shape to work, Pepper, let alone drive. You need medical attention. And rest. When's the last time you ate?"

She scoots back on the couch again, gritting her teeth with the effort. Her normally reddish complexion is gray and mottled. The room is dreary. I turn on a lamp. Pepper blinks.

"The first thing you need to do is tell Pence and everyone else what really happened. Tell them you made up the story about wrecking your car to throw Badger off and to buy yourself some private time to recover. You know what happens to cops who lie. They have no credibility, they can't testify in court. If you can't testify in court, you'll be fired. People need to know what really happened to you, Pepper. And you need protection. You could still be in danger."

"Not gonna happen. They're done with me. As soon as you got Badger what he wanted they tossed me out on the street."

"I didn't get Badger what he wanted." Pepper's eyes pop.

"What do you mean?"

"He wanted a photo and an address. I only gave him a photo. And it's not real. It's photoshopped."

"I don't fucking believe you."

"I'm telling the truth. You need protection. And rest. And counseling."

"They won't get away with what they did to me."

"And you need time off."

"What I need is twenty-four hours, a car and I'm back in the saddle. Open for business. Ready to go."

"Pepper. I need you to listen carefully. I'm serious. If you don't voluntarily take time off, I'm going to put you off as unfit for duty. I'm a psychologist, I have a duty to warn if I believe someone is a danger to themselves or others."

"Unfuckingbelievable. First you fuck me over by keeping secrets. Now you're going to fuck me over by putting me off work? I thought you were my friend."

This is a surprise to me, but I need some leverage, so I go with it.

"I am your friend. Friends don't let friends work after they've been terrorized by a gang of thugs. We're getting ahead of ourselves. First things first, I don't care what you say, I am going to make you something to eat."

***

I hate electric stoves because they never get hot enough. I'm trying to make omelets with three eggs, the edible half of a moldy onion and some milk that barely passes the sniff test. I cut the freezer burn off a stick of frozen butter, throw it in the pan along with the onion and wait for it to cook. I hear Pepper in the bathroom and hope I haven't been conned into letting her shower only to have her climb out the bathroom window. My phone vibrates across the countertop with a text from Pence asking about Pepper. I text back, "A-OK."

The shower turns off. I poke at the onions to make certain they're soft, turn off the stove and walk into the living room to wait for Pepper to get dressed. I pick up a photo of Pepper and her parents, both of them tall and patrician looking. Her mother's light hair is swept back and up. She's wearing a tan skirt and a tailored blouse that tastefully reveals a near perfect model-like figure, slender yet womanly. Her father is dressed in white slacks and a dark blazer with an ascot tied at his neck, yacht club style. Pepper looks cold and awkward in a dark blue speedo, her red hair sticking out from under a swim cap. A large medal hangs around her neck. Nobody's smiling. Or touching.

"That's the day I won a high school swim meet in the butterfly event. It was a big deal." Pepper stands behind me, wearing a KPD t-shirt, jeans and flip-flops. Her head wrapped in a white towel.

"If it was such a big deal, why are you all just standing there like mannikins? Shouldn't you look happy?"

Something twitches across Pepper's face. "Did I ever tell you how I got the name Pepper?" She unwraps the towel and scrubs at her hair. "Police Woman was my mother's favorite TV show.

She just loved Sergeant Pepper Anderson. Still does. Watches reruns on YouTube."

"Then she must be very proud of you, growing up to be a police officer."

"The Pepper she wanted, the one they both wanted, was Angie Dickenson, beautiful, sexy, feminine. Not some gangly, six-foot tall lesbian with big shoulders." She stretches the towel between her hands, wrapping one end around her fist. "It's okay. You don't have to say anything. Everybody knows, except for you and Pence."

She picks up another picture of her parents dressed in party clothes, her father in a tuxedo, her mother in a pale green ball gown. Looks at it and puts it back. "Pepper Anderson would have spotted the thugs who were following her. Ran them off the road. Handcuffed them. Hauled them off to jail. All without back-up. She wouldn't even get a run in her stockings."

"Pepper Anderson wasn't a real person or a real cop. You're both."

Pepper snaps her towel at the couch, knocking a pillow to the floor. "Here's what you don't get, Doc." She pauses, about to say something so profound she plants both feet firmly in place. "I let them get my freaking gun." Her words clack, one by one, like the wheels of a train. "It's the worst thing a cop can do. Once everybody finds out, I'm toast. No one will want to work with me. I wouldn't want to work with me. Nobody gives a shit that I'm queer, but they will give a shit that I'm weak. So, do it. Take me off duty."

She raises her hands in the air, the towel dangling like a white flag of surrender. "Those bastards were never going to kill me. Only scare me to death, so I'd scare you into finding Badger's son. Well, he got what he wanted. Big time. I'm scared of my own shadow. What am I going to do the next time some asshat tries to hurt me? Hand him my gun?" She snaps the towel again. "I could quit. Get a stress disability. Go back to school, get a teaching certificate. I could be a swim coach. And a vigilante. Go after those bums, myself. No one watching over my shoulder."

"Just because you lost a fight doesn't make you a bad cop. Do you think you're the only cop who ever lost a fight? Or a gun?" She doesn't answer. "You're not. You may feel like the only one because when it does happen, there's so much shame, nobody talks about it. Good cops lose fights. Smart cops lose fights. Strong, careful, hot shot cops lose fights. Know why? Because the bad guys know what they're going to do before the good guys figure it out. Bad guys don't fight fair." I walk to the bookshelf. Pepper's parents, frozen together in their silver frame, dominate the room like ruling monarchs. Pepper did the best she could under terrifying circumstances. Her inability to credit herself is a lethal mash-up of her parents' disdain with her own longing for their non-existent approval.

"What you have, Pepper, is an injury, a psychological wound. People recover from injuries. So will you. Sometimes, awful things like what you just went through, trigger old feelings of insecurity or helplessness. Your parents treated you like a performing seal, probably to shore up their own insecurities. I'm guessing that whatever you did, however hard you tried, nothing was good enough for them. I'm not judging you like they did. No one is. You did the best you could under extreme circumstances."

Pepper doesn't respond. She just stands in front of the photo rubbing her nearly dry hair like she's rubbing away bad memories. I can almost feel how much she's aching. Mom and Dad, disappointed and bewildered that their refined union had produced a child so far from their expectations that they could do little more than walk through parenthood, reciting their lines with cold, emotionless accuracy. All the ballet lessons in the world couldn't turn their ugly duck daughter into the delicate, feminine creature they craved. All she had was swimming. Swimming saved her life and brought her hope.

"Let me tell you something else, Pepper. Your parents missed out. Not only do I think you're a good cop, I would be proud to have you for my daughter."

I do what I can with the omelets, but the frozen waffles are so far beyond their expiration date they have no taste, even slathered with jam and butter. We eat in silence, too emotionally wrung out to talk. She stops me from washing the dishes and tells me to go, I've missed too much work.

"I'll wait until you start your car," she says. "This isn't over. Not for him. Not for me. Lock your doors."

I don't like what she's saying, but I'm happy to hear her cop-self rising to the occasion. She stands on the walkway in front of the door to her apartment and watches me walk down the stairs and across the parking lot. I walk, spine straight, head high, the key to my car wedged between my fingers like a weapon. It's only until I lock the doors to my car and start the engine that my heart begins to slow.

42

I head back to my private office. Blow through a stop sign, race past parking lots, car washes, cul-de-sacs, anywhere Badger's men might be waiting. I tell myself to calm down.

Badger's not after me. He has the photo Frank created. All I need to do is keep pretending to look for his son's address and eventually he'll give up. I'm such a fool. The Badger I remember, the funny, eager to please, affectionate kid I think is still reachable, doesn't exist, maybe never did. The real Badger, the man who kidnapped Pepper is cruel, evil, and damaged beyond repair. I pull into the parking lot as the alert tones on my cell phone blare like klaxon horns in a prison riot. I answer, expecting it to be Frank. Badger's voice, harsh as hinges on a rusty door, grates in my ear.

"Happy to see Pepper? It's only because of me that the crew didn't indulge themselves, if you know what I mean." I beat back a mental picture of what he means.

"How do you know where I am? How do you know I've seen Pepper?"

"Her early release is a good faith gesture of my gratitude for all you've done for me."

"Don't mistake what I did as a favor. The only reason I sent you your son's picture is because you forced me to do it, so you'd release Pepper."

"I'm grateful, I didn't even wait to get my son's address before I filled my end of the bargain."

"Do you expect me to thank you? Is that what you want? That photo of your son is all you're getting from me. Pepper's back, I'm finished trying to help you."

The door to my office building opens. Three of my colleagues walk by miming an invitation to join them for coffee. I wave, smile, and shake my head.

Badger's voice is so loud I have to hold the phone away from my ear.

"Doc, doc, doc. You're starting to piss me off. I don't think you want to do that."

I remember Charlotte's warning, word for word. "Watch your step. The last thing you want to do is piss him off." Charlotte was right. I don't want to piss Badger off, I want to strangle him.

"I'm living with savages, Doc. I could be dead tomorrow. I need you to find my son."

I hang up. He calls back. I pick up despite myself. "Pepper was easy pickings the first time. Think of how she would feel if my guys went for a second round. Don't forget your pal Eddie Rimbauer put me in the joint, turned me into a fucking cripple. You don't want to give me a reason to snatch his ugly ass, do you? Because if I do, what happened to Jerry will look like a walk in the park."

"What's happened to you?" I yell so loud the woman who is getting into the car next to mine turns to look at me. "The boy I remember had a heart."

"That little freak? He's dead. I killed him. He wouldn't have survived for a second in the joint."

"You killed Pixie, didn't you?"

"Me? I'm in prison. Locked up."

"You had someone else do it."

"I had to protect my assets. For my son. She was working for the cops."

"How did you know that?"

"What are you talking about? You told me. Sent me a text."

43

Tired as I am and deserving of sleep, all I can do is listen to Frank's breathing and replay the conversation with Badger. How can he think that I was the one who told him about Pixie? That's nuts. I did a lot of things wrong, but that's not one of them. The thing I did wrong, the thing that makes my skin crawl, is that I wanted so badly to find the good in him, I made it up. I stare at the shiny bits in the textured ceiling. The last time we talked about it, Frank promised to replace the ceiling with something more contemporary and then he mumbled about how the barber's kids always need a haircut and the shoemaker has holes in his shoes. I hate this ceiling, it looks like cellulite gone mad. Popcorn. Cottage cheese.

Cottage cheese? The last time I got close to that lumpy, miserable stuff, my mother and I were eating lunch at the food court. The day we went shopping for my wedding dress. The day Wendy and Mysti joined us and my mother, spellbound by their innocence, took Wendy on a shopping spree. I swing my legs over the edge of the bed, grab my robe and pick up the phone. Frank wakes up.

"What's happening? Why are you walking around in the dark with your telephone?" He turns on the light. "It's 5:00 a.m." He looks around the room, trying to get his bearings.

"Badger thinks I told him about Pepper's CI. I just now figured out who did. I have to call my mother. She's in danger."

"Your mother and Badger? Dot, stop. You're having a bad dream. Your mother is fine. She called tonight, we talked for thirty minutes. She was full of questions, as usual. Where were you? How are the wedding plans? She sounded fine."

I rush downstairs and call Badger on his cellphone. The call goes through without interference from the prison staff, no questions asked. I picture him sitting on his bunk, holding forth to his devoted followers—inmates and COs alike—king of his own prison fiefdom.

"Dr. Meyerhoff? With good news, I presume."

"It wasn't me who told you about Pixie. Someone used my mother's phone to call you. We have the same last name." There's a rumble in the background. Laughter. Talking. People moving. Glasses clinking. "Don't you dare touch my mother. She has nothing to do with this."

"Is that so? Wish you had called me earlier. I do hope my devoted followers haven't gone rogue on me." He disconnects.

Frank barrels down the steps, barefoot, in his pajamas and grabs me by the shoulders.

"Stop it. Talk to me. Tell me what's going on."

"I have to call my mother." I fumble at the phone, my shaking fingers landing on the wrong numbers. Frank takes the phone, punches in her number and hands it back to me at the first ring. Three more rings and it goes to voice mail.

"Hello. This is Rivka. Thank you for calling. I can't come to the phone right now. Your call is important. Leave a message at the tone and I'll return your call as soon as I am able." My mother sounds like she's reading from a script. Carefully following all the bullet points suggested by the phone company's brochure on voice mail etiquette. There's a brief pause. I can picture her, staring at the list of instructions, uncertain about how to end her message. "Okey, dokey," she says. I hit the pound key and advance to the message tone.

"Wake up Mom. Wake up. You're in danger. Call 911. I'll explain later. Ask for help. Lock your door and don't open it to anyone who isn't wearing a police uniform. Call me back so I know you got my message." I hang up.

"Dot, if your mother is really in danger, call the Pleasant Gardens security department, tell them what's going on and ask them to make a welfare check."

"You do it," I say, "And wait here until she calls back. I'm getting dressed." I run back upstairs. Frank follows. Watches me struggle into my jeans and a sweatshirt.

"Backwards," he says. "Your sweatshirt is on backwards. Slow down a little. Where are you going?"

I grab a jacket out of the closet. "To my mother's. Where did I put my damn purse?"

"It's hanging over the back of a dining chair, where you always leave it." He steps in front of me, puts his hands on my shoulders. "Stop for a second. Tell me why you think she's in danger."

"Badger thinks it was me who told him about the confidential informant, but it was Wendy. I just figured it out. Wendy used my mother's phone when they were shopping. Remember those hang up calls my mother was getting? I'll bet one of Badger's followers got her to give out her address. It wouldn't take much. All the caller would have to do is pretend to be from one of the zillion lost causes my mother supports."

"I still don't get it."

"Badger's furious because I told him I wouldn't look for his son anymore. He's going to kidnap my mother to force me to find his son. Just like he did with Pepper." I run out of breath. And words.

"This is a job for the police, Dot. Not you. This man is dangerous."

The phone rings. Frank picks it up, listens for a second and hands it to me. I don't care how angry she is that I woke her up, hearing my mother's voice will be better than winning the lottery and the Nobel Peace prize at the same time.

"Badger did a runner, broke out of prison." Pepper sounds like she's calling from another planet. I grab hold of a chest of drawers to steady myself. Tiny black dots swarm in front of my eyes.

"That can't be true. I just talked to him, minutes ago." Then I remember the rumbling noises in the background. Laughter, conversation. The clink of glasses.

"Where was he when you talked to him?"

"I don't know. I thought he was in his cell. When did he escape? How did he escape?" Frank offers me a mug of coffee. I push it away. I'm shaking so hard if I had any caffeine, I'd probably dislocate every bone in my body.

"Yesterday. He must have a guard on his payroll. Snuck out of the furniture workshop inside a mattress that was being delivered somewhere. Driver got hijacked, knocked out cold. When he came to, all the mattresses were lying in the road, one of them was sliced down the middle. Stuffed with Styrofoam pellets."

"Badger's going after my mother. I've tried numerous times to get her on the phone. No answer. When you called, I thought it was her calling back."

"What's your mother got to do with Badger?"

"Wendy used my mother's cell phone to warn Badger about Pixie. The caller's name on the phone was Meyerhoff, same as mine. He thought it was me doing him a favor."

"How did Wendy get your mother's phone?"

"My mother and I met her by accident at the mall when we

were eating lunch. After lunch, I went back to the office and my mother took Wendy shopping for a birthday present for her daughter. That must have been when it happened. I'm terrified Badger had someone trace her address through her cell phone number. I'm going to look for her."

"Don't do that. You just said your mother's not answering her phone. I don't want you running into Badger's flunkies. How did Wendy know about Pixie? That's restricted information."

"Tom told her." I hear Pepper inhale. "Wendy said he was hanging around dispatch, flirting, talking about what a great cop he is. That he'd never use a CI like you did because they're unreliable."

"Do you believe her?"

"I don't know who to believe any more."

"I need to talk to Wendy in person."

"Pepper, you're still injured. You can't drive."

"Tell your husband to call KPD as soon as we get off the phone, get them to start looking for your mother. Then pick me up. We're going to the detention center to talk to Wendy and we're taking Tom with us."

44

Frank watches me back out of the garage, drive over a curb and head out of the cul-de-sac, tires squealing. The sky is pitch black and the streets are empty save for a few lonely commuters hoping to beat the traffic. I blow a stop sign. A car careens past on two wheels, horn blaring as the driver gives me a one-finger salute.

My mind is swirling with dark thoughts. My mother's broken body, beaten, murdered, tossed on the side of the road. Frank breaking our engagement. Pence firing me. My once happy life in shambles, an orphaned spinster on the public dole.

I edge my way into a line of commuter traffic as a wan sun struggles behind the early morning fog. The metering lights are on. I inch forward toward the entrance to the freeway. My car dwarfed by oversized corporate shuttle buses carrying tech workers to and from their jobs, their faces hidden behind tinted windows. I imagine the passengers, snug in their reclining seats, curled around their electronic devices. A throaty blast rouses me and I scoot forward onto the freeway, wedging myself into traffic, an ant trying to keep pace with a herd of galloping giants.

Pepper is standing by the front door to her apartment, leaning over the railing, her head swiveling in all directions. The cuts and bruises on her face still visible. She starts down the steps the minute she sees me. Head down. One step at a time. Her hand on the railing like an old woman. She doesn't say a word as we drive to Tom's house.

Tom answers the door. He's rumpled, sleep deprived, barefoot, wearing only a pair of pajama bottoms and his duty weapon.

"What the hell time is it?"

I tell him it's almost 7:00 a.m. He motions us inside. We tip-toe down a short hall to a kitchen so large and filled with shiny stainless-steel appliances, I feel like a prisoner in a Crate and Barrel catalogue.

My mother, apparently abandoning her life-long dedication to anti-consumerism, wants Frank and me to sign up for a wedding registry. Tell our friends and relatives what we need and how much it would cost them to fill our greedy dreams. Sophie's granddaughter did this and got everything she asked for. Plus, it makes it so much easier for the wedding guests. They don't have to shop. They don't have to guess. They don't have to think. I told my mother to tell Sophie that wedding registries may be great for a young couple starting out in life, but Frank and I have too much stuff accumulated from one too many weddings. We don't want any gifts we can't eat, drink, or burn.

Tom takes a coffee pod carousel out of a cabinet and spins it around. "Take your pick. I got every flavor in the world." He pours water in the machine and presses a lever. There's a gurgling sound, then a hiss.

"Glad to see you, Pepper. We were worried. Heard you crashed your car. At least that's what the chief is telling everyone. You do look banged up."

"I'll live."

"Are you going to tell me why you're here?" He turns his back, fusses with the coffee.

"Badger broke out of prison yesterday. Why didn't you call me?"

"You're on medical. Pence said nobody should bother you."

"Then why didn't you call *me*?" I ask. "I'm not on leave."

"Why would I call you?"

"So I could protect myself. And my mother."

"The Doc thinks Badger has kidnapped her mother, like he kidnapped me." Tom startles, sloshes the coffee in his cup, but doesn't say anything. "We don't know this for sure, so we're going to interview Wendy, who appears to be Badger's personal source of information. We thought you might like to come along since you're Wendy's personal source of information."

Tom's face turns as purple as the fruit bowl he almost knocks off the counter.

"What the hell are you talking about?"

"Wendy told me you were hanging around dispatch," I say. "Flirting, bragging, talking about how you'd never use a CI like Pixie because CIs are unreliable."

"You believe that little shit? She's a pathological liar. Been lying to us from the get-go. She'd turn her mother in to cover her tracks." His breathing accelerates, his bare chest rising and falling in rapid succession. "I need a minute to get dressed, tell MaryAnne where I'm headed and then let's get going. The sooner we do, the faster we straighten this out."

Pepper goes out to the car while Tom gets dressed. I call Frank who is staying home from work, waiting by the telephone in case my mother calls. He answers on the first ring. "Nothing from your mother. The police are on their way to her condo." I tell him Pepper, Tom, and I are going to the county detention center to interview Wendy. He asks me if I'm scared. I tell him I couldn't be safer, surrounded as I am on two sides by armed police officers.

I leave out how my brain feels like a multiplex movie theater with rotating horror flicks. My mother terrified, tortured, dead. Badger, armed to the gills, willing to do anything to protect an empire he has created for a son he has never met.

45

Wendy is waiting for us in an interview room, drinking coffee and chatting up two deputies. Their faces go somber the minute they see us.

Wendy smiles like a restaurant hostess. Tom doesn't waste a second.

"How do you get off telling the Doc that I told you about Pepper's CI? It never happened. You heard it from Eddie. Right? How much did the two of you get for telling Badger? Big pay day?"

"You did. You're the one who told me."

"I did not."

"I have it on tape."

Pepper smiles slightly and tries to hide it.

"Sit down, Tom," I say. "You can sort this out later."

"I want to get to the bottom of this now. My reputation is on the line."

"So is my mother's life. Wait your damn turn." I pull up next to Wendy and sit, eye-to-eye. "Listen to me carefully. I need your full attention and your complete honesty." She starts to talk. I shut her down. "Did you use my mother's cell phone when the two of you were shopping for Mysti's birthday present?"

"Yes. I did." She straightens her back, the honest broker of known facts. "I didn't think it was a problem. My phone was dead. I had to call my mother to tell her when Mysti and I would be home. I didn't think your mother would mind. I can pay for the call if that's what she wants."

"Did you call anyone besides your mother?"

"Like who?"

"Did you call Badger about Pepper's CI?"

Little pulses start to throb at her temples and throat. "You know I told Badger about Pepper's CI. I already told you I did. Do I need a lawyer?"

"You can have whatever you want, Wendy," I say. "Except placement in a prison where you get to see your daughter every week. Because I'm going to tell the judge you're a pathological liar and an unfit parent whose daughter belongs in a foster home." I muster my best imitation of command presence. "I'll ask you one more time, whose phone did you use to tell Badger about Pixie?"

"What difference does it make whose phone I used?"

I slap my hand on the table. Coffee splashes out of Wendy's cup onto her lap. She backs up making a big show of wiping off her jailhouse jumpsuit. I lean over the table and grab her wrists. The edges of my fingernails dig into her skin. She sits up, straight as a stalk of corn. Pulls her hands free and rubs her wrists.

"I'll tell you why it matters," I say in a voice I don't recognize. "Badger's kidnapped my mother." Little Miss Innocence makes the sign of the cross and I see her for who she is. A wrecking ball of a human being whose moral compass has only two points, in trouble or out. "If you hadn't used her phone, Badger wouldn't have known my mother existed."

"I'm so sorry." She starts to cry. "Why did he take your mother?"

"He's trying to force me to do something for him."

She locks onto our shared predicament. "That's exactly how he is with me and Weejay. It's what I've been telling you. He was always forcing me to do something and then threatening to hurt Weejay if I didn't do more. I wanted to stop. I really did. But Weejay told me Badger was going to kill him if I didn't keep giving him information." She gulps a mouthful of air, chokes, tries to keep talking.

"Weejay's still not safe," Pepper steps in, talks over Wendy. "He's in the Lakeville Detention Center. It's just a small rural jail. Not a lot of security. If you don't cooperate with us, I'm going to tell Badger where Weejay is. Then Badger's going send one of his thugs to get your husband. Simple. The guy gets busted for something minor. A few nights in jail. Just long enough to stick a knife in Weejay's back or strangle him. Or beat him over the head with a sock full of rocks. Is that what you want?"

Wendy chokes again on a mouthful of air and tears. "No." It's almost a howl. "I love him. He loves me. He's sick and he's scared."

Wendy's desperation makes me cringe. I can only hope Badger is as desperate to connect with his son. Desperate enough to believe me when I bring him a phony address, because I don't know what else to do to get my mother back.

"If you cooperate, I can get the chief to transfer Weejay someplace safe, but only if you cooperate. Up to you." Pepper is cool, composed, totally in control.

"What do you want me to do?"

"Write a letter to Badger," I say. "Tell him you were the one who warned him about Pixie, not my mother, not me."

"I'm not good with words."

"Au contraire, Wendy. I think you've been talking circles around us for weeks." Pepper jostles the edge of the table with her knee.

"Not to worry," I say. "I'll dictate, even help you spell." I hand her a piece of paper and a pen. She picks it up, looks at it like she's never seen a pen before. "If WeeJay gets killed, Wendy, Mysti will have to go through life without her father. Is that what you want?" She shakes her head, starts to write. "And I have a mother," I say. "At least you better pray I still do. Old as I am, I need her in my life. She's going to walk me down the aisle."

46

"Don't talk. Eat." Fran stands in front of Pepper and me, commando style, hands on her hips. I swallow some eggs, take a bite of toast and start to talk. "Two more bites," she barks.

"I'm not a child."

"You could have fooled me," she says without moving. Eddie pours more coffee into my cup. Then into Pepper's. We drove here after the interview with Wendy, both of us starving.

"I can't eat while you are staring at me." I shove my breakfast plate at Eddie who backs away like I've offered him a dish of scorpions.

"Clean your plate. There are kids starving in China," he says. "Badger has kidnapped my mother." I think I've already said this six times.

"Everyone in the state is looking for your mother," Fran says. "It's all over the news. You need to be somewhere safe. Finish your food. Then go to the police station."

"Or you can stay here." Eddie lifts his apron to show me a gun, the one he "forgot" to turn in when he retired. "If Badger comes by, I'll make sure he's gets lead poisoning instead of food poisoning." His hand forms into a mock pistol. He's terrified of Badger and covering it up with self-deprecating humor. He put Badger in prison, turned him into a human rocking horse.

Fran whacks him on the butt. "Stop it. This is serious. He could be after you too, you know."

"I want to go home. I need to talk to Frank. Stay by the phone."

Pepper stands. "I'll go with you. Make sure you get home safely. Plus, I'm not too cool about being alone the rest of the day."

Frank ushers Pepper and me through the front door, scans the street and clicks the locks closed. We hug hard without speaking. There's a baseball bat, a sledgehammer, and a fireplace iron leaning against the wall. I don't have to ask why.

Frank has a brief report about my mother. The Pleasant Gardens security officer thinks my mother has cognitive problems, sundowner's syndrome he called it, and simply wandered off. I start to ask where the security guard got his psychology degree when Frank stops me because he's not finished saying what he needs to say. He called KPD after Pepper and I left the house and doesn't give a crap if I never speak to him again, because, if I'm dead, there will be no talking at all.

"The last thing I want is for KPD to show up, guns blazing. All we'll get out of that are dead officers and a dead mother. I have a letter from Wendy, a confession that she was the one who told him about Pixie, not my mother. I'm going to call Badger, make a deal, show him the letter and then promise to bring him his son's address after he lets my mother go."

Pepper steps between me and Frank. "He broke out of prison. He has no reason to keep his end of the bargain."

"He released you, didn't he? The best predictor of future behavior is past behavior."

Frank grimaces "So now we're back to under all that ink lives the cute little boy he used to be? He's not that boy now. He's an evil sonofabitch who killed two people. He won't think twice about killing you or your mother."

"All he wants, all that makes him feel like he hasn't wasted his life, is his son. It's the only leverage I have."

"Bad idea, really bad idea," Pepper says.

Frank claps her on the shoulder. "I'm with her. Listen to the professionals."

I remind them both that I'm also a professional. I may have screwed up with Badger, but that doesn't erase two decades of practice as a psychologist. People are complicated, not monolithic. I have to believe that or I'm in the wrong profession. I excuse myself on the pretext of wanting to shower and change clothes, lock myself in the bathroom, turn on the water and call Badger.

"Let me speak to my mother."

"What makes you think I know where your mother is? I'm not even sure where I am." His voice is slurred.

"I have an address where you can write to your son. After you release my mother."

"Other way around. You get me what I want and then I'll see. Maybe your mother won't want to be released. It's been a while since she's been around young studs. I think she's enjoying the attention."

"Don't you touch her. Don't you let anyone touch her."

"Hey, you're breaking my fucking eardrums." He mumbles something to someone in the background. I hear a woman laugh. "Think about it, Doc. How's she going to eat or piss without someone touching her to untie her hands? But don't worry, I'm a sensitive guy. I got her a chaperone." More laughter. None of it my mother's.

"Let me talk to her."

"No can do."

"How do I know she's still alive? Or that if I get you what you want, you'll release her?"

"You don't. You have to take my word for it. Just like I took your word, only you let me down. Lied to me. My bad for trusting you. But I wised up, got your feisty old mamma for insurance." I hear more rumbling and laughing in the background.

My lack of options—get Jake's address or Badger kills my mother—makes the decision easy. I can worry about protecting Jake and Charlotte in the future. Right now, all I care about is getting my mother back alive.

"Where are you holding my mother? If I'm going to bring you your son's address I need to know where to bring it."

He yells at someone. I can't hear what he's saying. There's a small commotion before he puts his buddy, Mr. Raspy Voice on the phone. Raspy Voice gives me directions to a place somewhere in the Santa Cruz mountains and hands the phone back to Badger.

"Come alone, no cops."

"The police already know you have my mother."

"So? You're the only one who knows where we are. Keep it that way. Don't let me see any cops or you'll see your mother's head on a platter with her foot stuck in her mouth." I blink the image away.

"Something else you should know. I'm not going back to prison. Ever. A very liberating decision. Frees me up to do anything I want to anyone I choose. I like your mother. She's a cute old gal. Must have been a number when she was young. Don't make me do something I don't want to do." There's more shouting. "Sorry for the noise. I'm celebrating my vacation from prison with a few friends." He hangs up.

As soon as he disconnects, I call my social worker friend Laurie. She answers on the first ring. I tell her I need to talk to Charlotte, Badger's ex. Plead for her help. She tells me Charlotte and Jake have been "relocated."

"As in kidnapped?"

"As in assisted by an underground organization of women who help victims of domestic violence move out of state or out of the country. I don't know where they are. Charlotte said to give you a message if you called again."

"What message?"

"Be careful."

I dump some water on my head to make it look like I've showered, change my clothes, and go downstairs. Frank and Pepper are in the kitchen drinking coffee.

"Pepper," I say. "I need you to do me a favor. Open a post office box in Kenilworth, under the name of Charlotte Stebbins, Badger's ex-wife."

"Why can't she do it herself?"

"Because I don't know where she is."

"Why do you need a P.O. box? Do you know where Badger is? Where he's holding your mother?" She frowns. "You do, don't you? You talked to him. Just now. You weren't in the shower." She yanks her cellphone out of the back pocket of her jeans. "Where is he? I need you to tell me now."

"You've been in our bathroom talking to that monster? I don't freaking believe this." Frank pushes back from the counter. "You're not going anywhere. He'll kill you. Tell Pepper where he is."

Pepper crosses the room. Stands so close to me I can feel her breath on my neck. "I'm a hostage negotiator. I trained for this. You didn't."

"What are you going to do to stop me? Waterboard me? Use

your taser? Badger wants me, no one else. He's on a suicide mission. He talks about dying all the time. He's not going back to prison. He made that very clear on the phone. I think he's looking to go out in a blaze of glory, suicide by cop. This is my mother, my problem. I started it."

"I'd give a month's vacation to be the lucky cop who gets to take Badger out. He should be dead. Save the taxpayers a shit-load of money feeding his ugly face."

"You want to kill him because of what he did to you, Pepper. Don't give him that option. If he forces you to shoot him, you'll have his bloody image in your head for the rest of your life."

"I'd rather have Badger's death on my conscience than yours. That's what's going to happen if you try to get your mother back on your own."

"You think he's just going to hand her over?" Now it's Frank crowding me. "He's a sadist, he likes to torture people and doesn't have the guts to do it himself. He's vermin. Get real, Dot. You are no match for this man. You're going to get killed."

I push past them and reach for my coat. "I'm out of here. Every minute I spend arguing with you two, God knows what is happening to my mother."

Pepper blocks my way. Stands in the doorway, her long arms wide. Frank grabs me by my shoulders and steers me back toward the kitchen. "I don't care if I have to knock you out and help Pepper handcuff you to a chair, you're not going anywhere without police protection."

"We'll get your mother back, I promise," Pepper says. "Just not your way."

What does one wear to a kidnapping? Slacks? Sensible shoes? Pants with pockets? Pepper has taken my car and gone back to the station to confer with Pence, SWAT and the negotiating team. Frank and I sit in silence, staring at the floor, waiting for Pepper to call. We're holding hands. Every five minutes, he asks if I need anything. When the phone rings, we both jump.

47

The place where Badger is holding my mother is tucked away in the hills above an exclusive enclave for Silicon Valley's millionaire prodigies. Their spectacular hightech homes cheek by jowl with the faux French half-timbered mansions of the old money horse set. Frank insists he drive and I let him, relieved to have a little more time to torture myself with the million awful scenarios that are playing in my head.

"Tell me again," he says after twenty minutes of silence. "What's the plan?"

"We've already gone over it twice."

"Then let's do it a third time."

"I walk to the door. Hand Badger his son's phony address. He hands me my mother, who looks unharmed and happy. She and I get into the car and you drive off into the sunset."

"Goddamnit, Dot." He pounds the steering wheel. "This isn't funny. I'm scared shitless."

"Me too," I say as we pull next to a battered metal mailbox attached to a tilted two by four. "We're here."

The mailbox sits at the end of a steep rock-strewn dirt track leading into a woody lot. Pepper has told Frank to stay on the road, drive ahead, park out of view. Whatever he does, not to pull up directly in front of the house. He drives forward a few yards, puts the car in park and leaves the motor running for a quick getaway. I start to scramble out the passenger door. He grabs my hand and leans in to give me a kiss.

"Be safe. I love you."

"I love you back." Our fingers touch for a second and slide apart.

At the top of the track is an old white barn surrounded by sagging fences. A spindly pine forest runs along the back and side. There's a pile of cut wood near the front door. A thin line of gray smoke rises from a metal pipe jutting through a ragged hole in the roof. I take a step. My legs are shaking. The track rises in front of me like Mt. Everest, the Death March to Bataan, and the Navajo Long Walk down the Trail of Tears. I tell myself to stop being dramatic. All I need to do is put one foot in front of the other and keep my eyes on the ground. I'm safe, I'll be okay. There's a gear-strapped cop hiding behind every tree, every rock, in every gully. Their faces blackened, heads covered, rifles pointed.

Badger is waiting for me. Standing in front of a battered sliding wood door that's fallen off its rails. He's wearing jeans, a tank-top, and a gun. It's the first time we've been face-to-face with no correctional officers, no shackles.

"You alone?"

"Yes."

He squints and turns his head, scanning the woods. I hold my breath. "Where's your car?"

"Parked on the road. I didn't want to get stuck in one of these." I nudge my foot along a deep crevice filled with pine needles and rocks. "Where's my mother?"

He gestures for me to precede him inside. Staggers a little as he turns. The barn is lit by scattered battery-operated camping lights that gleam like stars in a dark sky. The air smells of moldy hay, horse manure, and the pungent odor of methamphetamine. Badger stumbles over a pile of empty pizza boxes and beer bottles. The clatter of falling glass echoes through the room. A woman's voice calls out from the back.

"You alright, Badge?"

"Okey-dokey," he says and turns to me with a smile. "How 'bout a beer?" He uncaps one for himself, clearly not his first.

"Where's my mother?"

"Let's see what you got."

"Not until I see my mother."

His smile disappears. "Don't make me slap the shit out of you, Doc."

"Do what you have to do, just release my mother. Here . . ." I hand him a piece of paper with the phony P.O. box written on it and a copy of Wendy's confession. He walks to a camping light, his rolling gait accentuated by the uneven floor. He picks the light up by its handle and holds it over the letter.

"No shit. So, it wasn't you who tipped me off. It was that little prick WeeJay's bitch." He yells at someone I can't see. "Fuck me, I kidnapped the wrong woman." He turns back. "No problemo, WeeJay doesn't care about his wife. Plus, he doesn't have a dime to his name. Looks like I caught a lucky break. You love your mommy and you're rolling in dough." He smiles benevolently. Takes a long slug of beer. "That picture of my son you got me? He's my fucking spittin' image. Looks just like me when I was a kid. Handsome, dude. Gonna make me proud."

It's like Frank said. People see what they want to see. Badger wanted to see his son and he did. Thank you, Frank. Thank you, Photoshop. Thank you, human frailty.

"You have what you want, give me my mother."

"Now where did I put her?" He closes his eyes and scrunches his face in a mockery of deep thinking. "Hope she ain't lost."

He gives a loud whistle. "Ally ally in come free." A figure emerges out of the shadows at the back of the barn taking slow, deliberate steps. Even in the dim light I recognize the glint of Stell's bejeweled sandals and the soft contour of her velour jogging suit.

"Your grandson, Stell. Ain't he a chip off the old block?"

"Badger is your son?"

"Foster son. It was an informal arrangement. He didn't like the home the cops found. We stayed in touch."

"Where's my mother?"

"Out back. Babysitting the Sammies."

"I want to see her."

"In a minute," Badger steps between me and Stell. "My guys will be back soon. They're on a run, getting me more dope, some women. Your mother wouldn't want to leave without telling them goodbye. Have a beer, I insist." He bends over, his back to me and starts digging in the ice chest.

I calculate my options. Badger's drunk and stoned, limping like a rocking boat. Stell's wearing cheap sandals, no match for my running shoes. I promised Pepper I wouldn't make a move without police backing, but this may be the only opportunity to get to my mother before Badger's friends return and we have a blood bath. I start edging my way nearer the back door. One carefully placed step at a time. Badger spins around and fires his gun in the air, freezing me in my tracks.

There's a movement to my right. A slight rustle, no louder than a barn cat chasing a mouse. I see Pepper in the shadows. Dressed in black. Straight-armed, gun pointed at Badger, side-stepping her way around the edge of the room followed by a line of black-clad figures.

"Drop the gun." Pepper's voice knifes through the air. "On the ground, both of you, on your stomach, arms out to the side. Do it now."

Stell drops to the floor. Badger starts walking toward Pepper. "Is that you, Red? Welcome to the party."

"Stay where you are. Drop the gun."

"I think you already know my guys. They'll be here in five. They're gonna be delighted to see you. Finish what they never started."

Pepper's laugh is shrill, sharp and loud. "Open your eyes, you bastard. There's cops all over this place, inside and out, except for the ones taking your buddies to the slammer. Don't believe me?" Pepper bends her head to her shoulder mike. A second later police sirens shriek in response and for a moment the room is strobed in red and blue lights. Then all goes quiet again.

Badger shifts from one foot to another, squinting into the darkness. "No donuts, guys," he yells. "Plenty of beer. Come on in. No charge." He turns in a half-circle, looking for Pepper. She feigns left, then right. "Think you can take me by yourself, Red?" he calls into the space.

"It would be my pleasure," she says and moves into a deep shadow cast by an overhead loft.

"I told the Doc I'm not going back to prison." He opens his arms. "Come on, be a hero. Shoot the bad guy. Save the day." He stumbles toward the spot where Pepper's voice still hangs in the air, pounding his massive chest with one hand. "Hit the target. I'm making it easy."

"Is that how you want your son to remember you?" I say to his back. "Shot dead in a stinking barn, face down in a pile of horse shit?"

"Still there, Red?" He waves the gun around. "How long you gonna wait? Never shot nobody before? Give me one to the head. Like shooting a watermelon. Messy but easy."

I can hear her breathing. Short and rapid.

"I saw your son, Badger," I say. "In person. He gave me a message for you."

He wheels around.

"He was at the woman's shelter with his mother. I never told you. On the playground. Your ex was talking to a social worker. I went out to him. He asked if I knew you, where you were, why you didn't write."

"Bullshit. He doesn't even know I'm alive."

"You're wrong. He knew I was talking to his mother about you. He's a smart kid."

"What's the message?"

It takes me a second to know what to say, what I would have said if what I was saying now was really true. "First, I told him I knew you and that you thought about him every day, but you couldn't write because you didn't have his address. But now, after this meeting, you would have his address and, for certain, you would write him a letter. And then he asked if I could get you a message."

I stop. Mind racing, but not cooperating. I need to be right about this. There's too much at stake. Something up in the loft flaps. Then settles.

"He said to tell you that he loved you." I talk slowly, trying to calm the quaver in my throat. "He wants to see you. I told him you'd be happy to see him. He could come anytime."

"You told him he could visit? You bitch. Are you crazy? I don't want him to see me. I'm a fucking freak." He walks toward me. The barrel of his gun looking as big as the entrance to the Holland Tunnel. "All I wanted was to write him a letter and leave him a pile of money. Now everything is fucked up and you just screwed your mother."

"Write to him. You'll see. I can help you."

"You think I don't know how to write? What to say? I've written him a million letters. His bitch of a mother tore up the ones that got to him. The rest are in a box in my cell."

I can see Pepper circling behind Badger. She signals me to shut up and move out of the way so she can take a shot and not hit me. I don't move.

"What do you tell him when you write?"

"The usual shit. Be a good boy. Go to college. Don't be like me."

"When he visits, you can tell him in person."

"I told you. I don't want him to see me. All I want is for him to know what I did for him. All the money I made for him. Just him. My boy." His voice cracks.

"Money doesn't equal love, Badger. And it doesn't make you a father. Your son needs you in his life now."

"Get away from me with that shrinky shit." Badger's turning in circles, looking from me to Pepper and back again.

"You tried to contact your father when you were twelve. He didn't respond. It broke your heart. One year later, you were arrested for the first time. Don't you see the connection? Break the chain while you can. Don't treat your son the way your father treated you. If you do, chances are he'll end up the same way you have."

Badger groans like I've just stabbed him in the heart he's tried to cover with muscle and ink. He brings the gun up to his temple. Then under his chin. Then back to his temple. Now he's moaning like an injured animal, wild and heartbreaking. "Fuck it," he says more to himself than to me and flings his gun into the shadows. It hits something wooden and thuds to the floor.

The room fills with cops, flashlights crisscross the timbered ceiling, over the loft and along the walls. Pepper is bent over, her hands on her knees, gasping for air. A door opens at the back of the barn. My mother walks in holding Frank's hand. In her other hand, she holds a three-way dog leash, one Sammy attached to each lead.

Outside, in the car, my mother comforts me, not the other way around. New lines have sprouted around her eyes and the corners of her mouth. She looks pale. Frank is walking next to the road, trying to untangle the Sammies who are pulling in different directions, chasing a cacophony of exotic smells.

"Please stop crying," my mother says. "They didn't hurt me."

"You must have been so scared."

"You think I've never been scared before? When you're a Jew, you're scared all the time, but you don't show it. Good training for being kidnapped."

"It's my fault."

"Fault, schmault, I don't care whose fault it is or why Badger thought it was you who called him on the telephone." She shushes me when I try to explain. "You're meshuggeneh, trying to rescue me. He would have released me as soon as he got news about his son."

"They never hurt you?"

"They broke my furniture."

"Who did?"

"The guys who said they were cops. They knocked on my door. Told me you had been hurt and were calling for me."

"They were not police officers. They work for Badger."

"I know that now. When they came, I checked my telephone. There were dozens of calls from you and Frank, just like they said."

"We were trying to warn you to call the real police. That you were in danger. They never hit you?"

"Do I look hit? Do you see bruises? Black eyes?" She holds out her arms, pushes up her sleeves, shows me her wrists. "Big as they are, those men wouldn't sneeze without instructions from Badger. He runs everything. And he's not a bad person, if you don't have to look at him."

"He's a terrible person, Mother. He's done terrible things."

"Some people only see the worst in others. Like your father. And it made him miserable. I've always practiced seeing the good in people, especially when they don't see it in themselves. Most people are a mixed bag. That woman Stell, for example, a very calculating person who loves dogs more than people. She only pretends to love Badger. She is just waiting around for his money. Anyhow, I'm happy you found his son for him. It's the motivation he needs to change his ways."

Frank taps on the car window.

"I'm going to find someone to call animal control to take these dogs."

"No," my mother rolls down the window. "I'm taking them. They were good company. If it wasn't for them." She chokes up and tries to hide it behind a coughing fit.

"Three dogs in your small condo?" Frank looks at me. I shrug.

"I think Sophie would like one, maybe even Iris. Dogs are good companions. They force you to get outdoors and exercise."

I lean against the seat back, totally drained, nothing left inside except an overpowering longing to curl up in bed with Frank and fall asleep. A patrol car, siren blaring, drives past. Stell's face is pressed to the window, searching for her Sammies. They don't give her a second look. Another patrol car backs out of the track, wheels spinning and races downhill, Badger's unbelievable bulk a mere shadow in the back seat.

48

At KPD's insistence and against her wishes, my mother is staying with us because her apartment is still a crime scene. She stomps up the stairs complaining that she is being kidnapped for the second time and falls asleep the minute her head hits the pillow. The fickle-hearted Sammies, now imprinted on my mother, snuggle against her feet.

I fall into bed without brushing my teeth. Frank sits on the edge. "I want police protection. For all of us. You, me and your mother."

I don't want to have this conversation now. I don't want any conversation. What I want is sleep.

"You think Badger's going to take this sitting down? That he's not going to come after you? You lied to him about his son. About bringing the SWAT team to get your mother. He must be in a rage."

"Badger's in jail."

"He broke out before. Remember? And he has minions on the outside."

"They've been arrested."

"All of them?"

"I don't know, Frank. I need to sleep. Let's talk about this in the morning. Please."

He stands up and walks away without our traditional good-night kiss. In the doorway, his back to me, he announces that he's going downstairs to check the locks. And maybe sleep on the couch.

The next thing I hear is pounding. I roll over. Frank's side of the bed is empty. Pale light fills the room. The clock says 6:30 a.m. I hear an unfamiliar high-pitched clamor, followed by my mother's voice congratulating the Sammies on their skills as watchdogs. I grab a robe and head downstairs. Frank, still in his pajamas, is wrestling the couch back from where he jammed it against the front door. I look through the living room drapes. Pence, dressed for a public appearance, is waiting on my front stoop next to Pepper, who is still in uniform. Frank opens the door.

"Good morning everyone. And a very good morning it is."

My mother gives me a sidelong look. Pence steps in front of her. She pulls her robe closed and tightens the belt.

"You must be Mrs. Meyerhoff. I'm so relieved you are safe and unharmed. You are a very brave woman. I intend to recognize your courage, officially and publicly."

My mother ducks her head and looks at him over the top of her glasses. I recognize the gesture as one of my own. Did I borrow it from her or she from me?

"Who is this *pisk*?" my mother says, using the Yiddish word for loud-mouth.

"This is Jay Pence, he's the police chief and my boss."

"Are you the one who let my daughter risk her life chasing dangerous criminals?"

This is not the response Pence was anticipating. "I'm sure you know better than I do that your daughter is very good at ignoring other people's directions and doing what she wants."

"Of course. Why would she do what she didn't want?" Her rhetorical question stuns Pence into momentary silence, a sure indication of a slow thinker not worthy of my mother's time. She walks into the kitchen. Frank follows. The Sammies scurry behind. Their nails scratching across the hardwood floor.

I look at Pepper. She's slumped on the couch fighting sleep. I take my mother's place in front of Pence. "So, are you going to fire me?"

"First off, I'm going to give Pepper the medal of honor." She gives him a weak smile. "Then I'm going to give your fiancé a citizenship award for notifying us about your mother's abduction and assisting the SWAT team in their rescue effort. Then I'm going to suspend Tom Rutgers for a month, maybe more, for his careless indiscretion. He's lucky I'm not going to fire him. After which I'll think of something to reward your bravery while overlooking your complete refusal to follow protocol."

I could use a bigger office at HQ but decide this is not the time to push my luck.

"Pepper showed extraordinary good sense and courage, especially after what she has been through. I'm grateful she disclosed what really happened to her and I am, for your information, overlooking how long it took her to do that. Had she not skillfully organized the tactical assault on Badger's hideaway, I might be planning a funeral instead of preparing for an interview on the national evening news."

Pepper and I exchange looks, reading each other's thoughts. She's not getting an award for bravery, she's being honored for getting Pence on national TV. The smell of coffee fills the room followed by Frank carrying a tray of coffee mugs, followed by my mother with cream and sugar, followed by her canine entourage, all wiggles and wagging. Frank sets the tray on a table.

"Chief Pence," Frank's back is ram rod straight. "I don't know how much you know about what took place in the barn. The photo Dot gave Badger of his son is a mash up of an old photo of Badger as a kid. I photoshopped it myself. Badger is going to want revenge. I need protection for Dot, her mother and myself."

My mother glares at me. "That wasn't his son in the picture? You lied?"

"I would have told him anything," I say. "He was going to kill you."

"Still might," Frank mutters, loud enough for all of us to hear.

Pence puts his coffee down. "I fully understand your concerns, Mr. Hollis, but let me put you at ease. Put everyone at ease." He does a quarter turn to face Pepper. "Thanks to you, we picked up almost all of Badger's men. There may be a few still out there, but they are pretty much emasculated without Badger at the helm."

"That's not how I see it," Frank's voice is so sharp it sends the Sammies under the couch. "He's been running a major criminal operation from inside prison. Locking him up doesn't mean he's stopped giving orders to people on the outside."

"There will be a major investigation at Bradenton. Clearly Badger had inside help in his escape. No question about it. Badger may not have torched Jerry's trailer himself or beat that young woman to death with his own hands, but he is clearly responsible for ordering their murders. As of this morning, he's being transferred to Cherry Point, a maximum-security prison from which no one has ever escaped. He'll be in solitary confinement. No communication with the outside world."

"Mazel tov, congratulations," my mother says as she clinks coffee mugs with all of us. Frank looks at me. I look at my mother.

"I don't get it, mother. Yesterday you told me Badger wasn't a bad man. You were glad he was going to meet his son. Today, you're toasting his life-long incarceration. With no possibility of parole, he'll never see his son."

"I didn't say he was perfect. He made very bad decisions. But I don't need a PhD in psychology to know that when your father is a common criminal, your mother is a street walker, and you have the foster mother from hell, it's almost 100 percent guaranteed you won't make good decisions."

49

Dr. Rogoff is not happy with me.

"When I offer four sessions with a fifth at no cost if you're not satisfied with the results, I intend for those four sessions to be completed at the rate of one per week. Cognitive habits of positive thinking dissolve quickly without reinforcement and I cannot guarantee results when there are weeks between meetings."

"You do read the newspapers, don't you Doctor? Then you know that my mother was kidnapped by an escaped convict who had arranged the abduction of a Kenilworth police officer, the murder of her confidential informant, and was now attempting to pressure me into obtaining information about his son. A son he has never met because the boy's mother is so terrified of him, she and the boy have been in hiding for years."

"Still, you should have left me a message cancelling your sessions. I have other clients, equally troubled, who could have used your time."

"Are you deaf? Did you hear what I just said? My mother was kidnapped, almost killed!"

"Did you arrange this kidnapping yourself? To get your mother out of the way?" I am so flabbergasted by his question

I can't respond. "Answer my question, was it your fault your mother was kidnapped?"

I stand up. Start to put on my coat. "You know what, Dr. Rogoff? I'm wasting your time and I know for sure you're wasting mine. Not only do I not want the free fifth session, I don't even want this fourth one."

"Sit down. Don't run away from me. Or yourself. Answer my question. Are you responsible for your mother being abducted?"

I sit, my coat half on, half off. "I made a bargain with Badger and didn't deliver."

"Do I understand this correctly? You made a bargain with a deranged criminal?"

"He was desperate to contact his son, wanted his photo and an address. Instead, I gave him a photoshopped picture of himself and a phony address. Then I showed up to where he was holding my mother with the KPD SWAT team after I promised to come alone. Now he's going to spend the rest of his life in solitary confinement waiting in vain for his son to show up."

Rogoff grabs his chest. "Like a heartbroken golden retriever abandoned by his owner, his nose pressed to the window? When you got your PhD, Dr. Meyerhoff, were you also issued an X-ray machine that could read people's minds? And if so, may I borrow it?"

"Very funny. I get your point."

"I don't think you do. You sound as if you're responsible for this man's incarceration."

"Badger is a dangerous man, a damaged man. But that's not all he is. He had a rough start in life. Not the kind of start you recover from. Despite everything that's been done to him and all the bad things he did to other people, he loved his son, saved all his money to give to the boy so he could have a better life."

"Tell me again why any of this is your fault or your responsibility."

"Psychologists are supposed to do no harm."

Rogoff raises his hand, his index finger pointed at the ceiling. "Beneficence and nonmaleficence, harming and non-harming. I used to have two cats by those names."

"This is not funny. Stop making jokes."

Rogoff's bushy eyebrows tangle together. "From what you say and what I read in the newspaper, this man was a career criminal with delusions of power and fatherly grandeur. You know about fatherly grandeur, don't you? This man was and would be no more a father to his son than your father was to you. All either of them wanted and needed was an audience. In my opinion, giving blood money to this boy would only complicate whatever complicated feelings he already has for his father. I could hypothesize that you were projecting your own unmet needs for a father onto this Badger person and his son."

My coat falls to the floor.

"Shedding your skin? Good idea." He leans forward. "Let me be perfectly clear. I am very glad you and your mother came through this extraordinary experience safely, although I am dismayed to learn that you have inherited so much of your father's outsized ego. Who are you to think you can rehabilitate, let alone outwit, such a damaged individual? Not even the experts in criminal justice have been successful." He looks at me to make sure I'm following. "You obviously have a huge blind spot when it comes to your father. But what about your mother? I'm curious. Did you learn anything about her during all this chaos? Take your time. For once, think before you speak." He closes his eyes, his head tilted toward the ceiling, the picture of patience.

"I learned that my mother is a lot tougher than I thought.

And clever." He nods. "There was a lot I didn't know about how hard she had it being married to my father. She hid a lot of her suffering, for my sake, and did the best she could under circumstances beyond her control. Then and now."

"And who does that sound like?"

"I don't understand your question."

"Sounds a little like you, doesn't it? Muscling through. Never giving up. It's shocking to realize how much we ask of ourselves and how little control we actually have in life. When you accept your limitations and the reality of your situation, something neither your father nor this tormented criminal could do, life gets easier." He looks at his watch. "What else? Did you learn anything about yourself?"

I give this less thought than I imagined I would. "I learned that I have more guts than common sense. That my capacity for love is stronger than my fears. That I'm engaged to a man who would risk his life for me, even when he thinks I'm making a terrible mistake. That if I don't give everything I've got to this relationship, I'll regret it for the rest of my life."

Rogoff cups one hand inside the other, nods his head and releases a long, noisy sigh. I recognize the sound. It's the fatigue that accompanies listening with both ears and all your heart.

48

On my way home from Rogoff's office, I stop at Fran's. She and Eddie are huddled together in a back booth bent over the newspapers. Front page, above the fold, is a picture of Pepper in her dress uniform receiving the medal of honor from Pence. Frank and I and my mother are seated in the first row, where Pepper's parents should have been. Next to me, Raylene is resplendent in a black and white dress, her face glowing with victory as Pence announces the start of a new policy to require all dispatcher applicants to undergo pre-employment psychological screening.

"Lovely ceremony. Touching." Fran squeezes my hand. "Especially what Pepper said about you. About how much you helped her. How she wants to be a therapist when she retires."

"Oh God, not two of you." Eddie's face looks bloated and blotchy. Like he's been crying. Or drinking.

"With you around, Eddie, psychologists will never be out of work. Do you know what this idiot wants to do, Doc? If Wendy gets bail, and that's a big if, he wants to pay it."

"She needs help."

Fran punches him on the shoulder. "You're the one who needs help. Stop rescuing people and start taking care of yourself. From what I read in the paper, there are so many charges against little Miss Wendy, she'll be an old woman by the time she gets out of prison. Find better things to do with your money. Like save up for an apartment. Quit living in my storage room. And while you're at it, buy yourself some new t-shirts." Fran struggles out of her seat. "Fix him, Dot. I'm at the end of a very short rope."

"She's right, you know," I say. "You put yourself in a lot of danger. You have got to stop playing cop and rescuing people. Accept the reality of your situation. Find something else to do."

Eddie grabs my shoulder, pulls me forward, his mouth close to my ear. "I'm scared, Doc. I want a drink. I don't know how to be a civilian. All I know is how to be a cop. Fix things for other people. And I can't even do that right anymore. If I go back to drinking, I'm just committing suicide on the installment plan. I need a reason to live."

I push him back. "You have one and it's right in front of your face. Except you're too caught up in your own life to notice. Have you seen Fran's swollen legs? Her feet? How often she needs to sit down? Fran's been taking care of you your whole life. She's getting older. She needs help. It's time for you to return the favor. I don't think Fran can keep this place open without you."

He tilts his head, blinks like he's trying to see something off in the distance. "In plain English, what you're saying is 'Get off the cross Eddie, we need the wood.'"

"People love eating here. They love your abuse, the greasy food, the fact that this is a real place, not a corporate spinoff. Think about it. Where would young cops go if they didn't have Fran's? They feel welcome here with you and Fran behind the counter. There aren't too many places, these days, where a uniformed cop can get a meal without being stared at or harassed. Stay sober. Fran needs you. The cops need you. Wendy can fend for herself; it's what she's been doing all along."

49

Fran and Eddie are in the kitchen with Frank's sisters. Eddie's head is bent over a gigantic bowl of Iowa-style potato salad.

"Fucking A, this stuff is amazing." He blushes. "Sorry ladies. I don't know how to talk around normal people, too many years talking to cops and asshats. Sometimes one and the same." Frank's sisters, Rose, Violet, and Lily giggle. "This," he says to Fran, "is going on the menu. So is the Jell-O. All three versions, salad, dessert, and vegetable. And for police week, we're going to make the Jell-O blue."

Eddie's back on track. Taking more responsibility for running the café and taking better care of himself. Even bought a new sport coat and a half-dozen new t-shirts for the wedding. Fran too looks restored. This is the first vacation she's had in years. It's a new experience, having people cook for her, not the other way around.

My mother and Frank's mother huddle together on the couch, two animated apple dolls, discussing the provenance of an assorted pile of family heirlooms. When my mother explains that she doesn't have heirlooms because her family lost most of their possessions in the Holocaust, Frank's mother starts to cry and offers to share hers because now that the quote children are married, we are family.

Frank had warned his sisters and his mother about my red

wedding dress and they made me a bridal bouquet of fresh tomatoes and corn. They didn't really expect me to carry it, but it was so beautifully quirky, I insisted. We were married by a local judge on the deck of Lily's house, where we're sitting now, drinking iced tea. I can see Pepper in the distance, walking alone on a tractor trail. Her PTSD is settling, becoming more of a minor inconvenience than a major driver of her everyday life. Still, being in a crowd of strangers, even friendly strangers, takes its toll and she needs moments of solitude to calm herself and gather her thoughts.

"Where are you going for your honeymoon?" Frank's sister Rose pulls up an empty chair.

"The question is," Frank says, "Not where but when. We'll probably get around to it sometime near our fiftieth anniversary."

I poke him in the ribs. This is not the time nor the place to talk about the slew of depositions and trials we're facing as Wendy, Stell, and Badger fight their way through the justice system. Now is the time to listen to the corn growing—just like Frank told me, it actually squeaks—and revel in the safety of family.

Lavender plants perfume the air. Behind them, a trellis of green beans frames the fields, tidy rows of corn and soybeans, so long and straight they disappear into the horizon. After the wedding ceremony, my mother, arms locked with Frank's mother, looked out at the fields and toasted us with champagne. "Here's hoping that your lives together, as husband and wife, will be as straight and as long." Then the entire family raised their glasses to us and shouted "Mazel tov" at the tops of their lungs.

ACKNOWLEDGMENTS

No one writes a book alone. I am fortunate to have many outstanding resources, some of whom have been on the front lines for years. Michelle Perin, retired dispatcher, firefighter, and counselor; Sgt. Adam Plantinga; James L'Etoile, former associate prison warden (ret.) and author; retired police officer Dr. Joel Fay; police captain Alana Forest (ret.); Dr. Dave Corey; Communications director Mark Chase; author Ann Gelder; my cousin-in-law Kathryn Frank; my sister-in-law Doris Ober who has edited every book I've written; my friend and agent Cynthia Zigmund; the staff at BooksBNimble; and my forever husband Steve Johnson who puts up with me, even when it isn't easy, which is much of the time.

ACKNOWLEDGMENTS

ABOUT THE AUTHOR

Ellen Kirschman, PhD, is a police and public safety psychologist, a volunteer clinician at the First Responder Support Network, and a sought-after speaker and workshop facilitator. Kirschman has been awarded by the California Psychological Association for Distinguished Contribution to Psychology and the American Psychological Association for Outstanding Contribution to Police and Public Safety Psychology. She co-authored *Counseling Cops: What Clinicians Need to Know*; authored two self-help guides *I Love a Cop* and *I Love a Fire Fighter*; and writes a mystery series featuring police psychologist Dr. Dot Meyerhoff.

THE DOT MEYERHOFF MYSTERIES

FROM OPEN ROAD MEDIA